## SPLIT-SECOND REACTION

Longarm was quicker to draw than Vail. His answering shot came a fraction of a second before Vail's gun sounded. The man on the stairway triggered off another shot as his fingers cramped in his death throes.

During the fleeting instant when the muzzle-blasts of their two weapons flared, both of them had gotten another fleeting glimpse of the man who'd tried to cut them down. In the swift return of darkness, they heard his weapon clatter as it hit the floor.

Neither Longarm nor Vail spoke for a moment. Then Longarm said, "That son of a bitch made fools outta both of us, Billy. Now let's see if we can figure out who he is."

TABOR EVANS

# LONGARM

## AND THE ARIZONA SHOWDOWN

JOVE BOOKS, NEW YORK

LONGARM AND THE ARIZONA SHOWDOWN

A Jove Book / published by arrangement with
the author

PRINTING HISTORY
Jove edition / January 1992

ISBN: 0-515-10753-0

Jove Books are published by The Berkley Publishing Group,
200 Madison Avenue, New York, New York 10016.
The name "JOVE" and the "J" logo
are trademarks belonging to Jove Publications, Inc.

PRINTED IN THE UNITED STATES OF AMERICA

10  9  8  7  6  5  4  3  2  1

**AND THE
ARIZONA SHOWDOWN**

# Chapter 1

"Until last night, I was anxious to get to Denver," the young woman sitting beside Longarm in the Pullman coach seat said thoughtfully. "Now, I wish it was still a thousand miles away."

"Well, you won't have to wait all that much," Longarm told her. "We'll be there soon as the train gets to the end of this big curve."

"I didn't mean it that way," she protested. For a moment she sat silently, looking out the window.

Only the top rim of the bright glowing sun was visible now. The shadows cast by the western rim of the Rockies as the last rays of the slowly setting orb dropped behind them were lengthening across the ground.

"I'm both glad and sorry," she went on. "Glad because we're here and sorry because I know that when I leave tomorrow, you won't be on the train with me."

"You ain't a bit sorrier than I am, Jeanne," Longarm assured her. "It could be a lot worse if it wasn't for your train connections. I ain't forgot what you mentioned

1

about having to stay over here tonight."

"But you told me you'd have to report to your office as soon as we got to Denver," Jeanne protested.

"That was before we—well, before last night. But seeing as how you'll be here till your train leaves tomorrow, I sure ain't aiming to tell you good-bye till then."

Her frown deepening, she asked, "What's going to happen if you don't report to your office? When we were just getting acquainted, I remember you telling me that was the first place you'd have to go."

"Why, I wasn't saying I'd need to go to the office the minute I got off the train. Even if I wanted to, it's closed up now and won't open till the morning."

"And we can still be together tonight?"

"Why, sure. And more'n that. With you having to wait and catch that noon train, I'll have time to bring you back here to the depot and kiss you good-bye before I report in to my chief."

Longarm took his eyes off the girl when the locomotive's whistle sounded the two quick blasts that warned a stop was just ahead. Iron brake shoes began screeching, in a minor key at first, then with louder and more resonant grating as the train slowed and finally came to a halt at the depot platform.

Longarm stood up as he said, "Now, you just let me tend to seeing to your bags. Then—"

Jeanne broke in. "You won't need to bother with a lot of luggage. I've checked everything through to Chicago except that one little valise in the rack up there."

"That being how it is, we might as well get off," Longarm said. "I'll hail a hack and we'll have a bite to eat, if you're hungry. There's real fine restaurant in the hotel we'll be going to."

She smiled. "And I hope, a big fine bed instead of a cramped-up Pullman berth."

"Oh, sure." Longarm said as they made their way up the aisle toward the vestibule.

Most of the passengers had already left the coach, and they moved quickly, Longarm carrying the girl's valise. He turned when he reached the platform and offered his hand to Jeanne as she stepped down. She kept it in her grasp as they started away from the tracks toward the depot building. They'd just entered the building when Longarm stopped short. Jeanne looked up at him with a puzzled frown.

"Is something wrong?" she asked.

"I sure hope not," Longarm replied. "But I'm going to have to ask you to wait for me a minute. That fellow over yonder is my boss, Chief Marshal Billy Vail. Him being here looking for me can't mean nothing but trouble."

"Trouble for you?"

"Maybe, and maybe not. But I got to go see what he's come here for. It ain't like Billy Vail to wait around in the depot for a train to come in unless he's got business with somebody that's on it, and I got to be the somebody he's waiting for."

Longarm was bending forward to put Jeanne's valise on the platform as he spoke. From the door at the front of the depot building the report of a heavy-caliber pistol sounded, and Longarm heard the menacing whistle of its bullet just above his head an instant after he'd leaned down.

Before the echoes of the first shot had died away it was followed by a second, then a third. One was too high, the other too low; its slug screeched as it cut a groove along the depot's tesselated floor. Somehow neither shot found

3

a target in the roiling crowd of passengers.

Longarm grabbed Jeanne's forearm and pulled her with him to the depot floor as he dropped. His free hand was already reaching for his Colt, and even before they'd landed on the floor his eyes had been busy sweeping the area from which the shot had sounded, but he saw no one running toward the doors. Instead, the crowd was trying to push away from the openings.

Out of the corner of his eyes Longarm saw Vail swiveling around in the direction from which the shots had come. The chief marshal was drawing his revolver as he turned. He snapped off a shot and the slug chipped plaster beside one of the depot's doors. Then Longarm saw Vail lowering his weapon. From the look on Vail's face he knew the quick shot had missed its target.

Longarm had finished his draw before he and Jeanne landed in a sprawl on the floor. While they were still moving into a position that would allow them to rise, a second shot rang out, followed by an answering report from Vail's revolver. The chief marshal was also taking evasive action. Moving in a crouch, he was stepping spraddle-legged from side to side while his eyes were busy searching the doorway area, seeking the target he'd missed the first time and which had now disappeared.

Glancing around, Longarm saw movement aplenty in every direction, but none of the men he saw held a pistol. There was no one framed against the light coming through the glass panels of either of the big depot's broad doorways, nor could he see anyone in the crowded station who was hurrying toward a door. The passengers who'd been strolling toward the exits were still scattering, their moving figures blocking his vision.

"What on earth is—" Jeanne began.

4

"We've been getting shot at," Longarm told her. "And I don't know the whys and wherefores. But that fellow over yonder's my chief. He's been shooting back, so he oughtta know. Now, you just lay here by the luggage and stay quiet while I go find out."

"There isn't going to be any more shooting, is there?"

"Not likely," Longarm assured her. "And I wouldn't leave you by yourself if I figured there might be."

"Are you telling me that you don't have any idea why somebody would want to shoot you?" Jeanne asked.

"Oh, there's plenty of crooks on our wanted list that'd draw down on me anyplace I might happen to run into 'em. And my chief—the man I showed you just now— he's as likely a target as I am. That's why I need to go ask him if he got a look at whoever it was done the shooting."

"You think he can tell you?"

"Maybe so and maybe not. At this time of day it's likely all he'll tell me is to report in early tomorrow for some new case he's putting me on. Now if you'll excuse me, I'll be back in a jiffy."

"Of course. I'll wait right here."

Longarm took his cue from his chief's action. Vail had turned away from the outer doors and was heading toward him. Longarm took the few steps needed to meet him.

"You got any notion what that was all about?" Longarm asked when Vail came into speaking distance.

"Not the faintest," the chief marshal replied. "But just guessing, I'd say that whoever triggered off those shots had you in mind for his target. It's too bad I missed him, but he moved too fast for me to draw a good bead on him."

"Well, he wouldn't be the first one," Longarm said. "And he ain't the only one that's missed me either."

"I hope you got a good look at him," Vail said. "I didn't turn around in time to see anything but his back."

"Now, Billy, you know I wasn't looking at nobody but that young lady I got with me," Longarm told his chief. "And if you was in my place, you wouldn't've been gawking around either."

"I suppose not," Vail agreed. "Who is she, by the way?"

"Not that it makes no never-mind, but her name's Jeanne Fletcher, and I got acquainted with her on the train. But I guess you already figured that out."

"I'm not quite blind yet." Vail smiled wryly. "And knowing you, I'm past being surprised when I see you with a good-looking woman. She's not from Denver, is she?"

"She lives back east, but she's got to stop overnight here to change trains," Longarm said. "So those shots weren't aimed at her, if either you or me had any different ideas."

"Oh, there's no question about that gunhand," Vail agreed. "He had you in mind. But what I'm curious about is how he knew you were going to be on that particular train."

"Why, I imagine we'll find out sooner or later," Longarm observed. "Except it might be a little bit of a job, not knowing who he was or why he was potshotting me."

"I don't think there's too much we can do tonight to run him down," Vail said thoughtfully.

"Well, I got to agree with you on that, Billy," Longarm said. "But that ain't either here nor there. What I'm thinking about is how come you figured you had to meet me. Just guessing, I'd say you already got a new case for me, and you'll want me to get on it right away."

"It's not exactly a case," Vail told him. "Not yet, anyhow. I've just got Washington on my tail again, and I wanted to talk to you as soon as you got in."

"More talking than we could get through with here and now, I reckon?"

"Quite a bit more," Vail said.

"Go ahead and tell me," Longarm suggested. "I'm listening."

"It'd take too much time, and I'd like to tell you while I've got some papers handy. They're at the office."

"But, Billy—" Longarm began.

Before he could go on, Vail broke in. "Now, I'm not going to ask you to go back with me right now. I'll put it this way. After you and your lady friend get settled in, and you're sure she can get along without you for an hour or so, I'll ask you to meet me at the office."

"You're talking about tonight, I gather?"

Vail nodded. "It's that important, Long. I wouldn't be asking you if I wasn't sure."

"You ain't giving me much choice, Billy," Longarm said with a frown. "Not the way you put it. And I know you ain't giving me no bum steer. Let's call it a deal then. When do you expect me to be at the office?"

"I sure don't want to break in on what you've got planned with your lady friend, Long. Say you get there about midnight."

"That's when I'll be there then," Longarm agreed. "Now, I'll go back to Jeanne and see that she gets settled in, then I'll meet you at the office."

Without waiting to acknowledge Vail's approval, Longarm rejoined Jeanne.

"Judging by the look on your face, I don't suppose you found out anything from your chief," she said.

Longarm shook his head. "He didn't get any better look than I did at whoever it was done the shooting. But we better not waste our time standing here palavering." Bending, Longarm picked up Jeanne's valise and his own traveling kit. Then he went on. "There's a real nice hotel, the St. James, that ain't too far from the office. We'll get a hack outside and be there in a jiffy."

"Now that you've finished that shave you insisted on, I hope you'll take my invitation to join me," Jeanne said.

Longarm twisted his head as he looked at the mirror to inspect the last dabs of lather at the edges of the lines sculpted by his razor. He also looked at Jeanne, who was lying back, stretched out in the oversized bathtub. She was not looking at Longarm's back, but at his frontal image reflected in the full-length mirror on the bathroom wall opposite the tub.

Longarm returned the inviting smile Jeanne was flashing to him, then scraped away the last dabs of lather that remained on his tanned, rugged face. He wiped the razor's blade and laid it aside. Then he turned to face Jeanne. Though the water in the tub was slightly opaque from the soap she'd been using, it was clear enough for him to see the budded pink rosettes of her large firm breasts and the blurred outline of her dark pubic brush against her flawless ivory skin.

"Well, now, I ain't one to scrape a pretty face with whisker stubs, and I sure ain't about to make a lady take no for an answer when she invites me," he replied. "So

8

if you're sure there's enough room for the two of us, I'll just take your invitation."

Before stepping into the bathtub, Jeanne had pulled her glistening fall of dark hair into a flat bun at the back of head. She leaned back as Longarm stepped into the lukewarm water, and rested her head on the rim of the tub. When Longarm groped with his foot to find the bottom of the bathtub, Jeanne raised her legs slightly and parted them to allow him to place his feet between them.

Longarm kneeled and bent forward to press his lips on hers. Jeanne sighed as they prolonged the kiss. She wrapped her arms around his chest and pulled him close to her. Their tongues twined, darting and exploring. With the support of both his arms no longer needed, Longarm brushed his palm up Jeanne's side and slid it between their bodies to finger the firm budded tips of her generous breasts.

Jeanne's muscles quivered and grew taut as they held their kiss, and Longarm did not try to suppress the erection that was beginning. Now he could feel Jeanne's hand brushing down his rib-cage and sliding between their bodies. When her fingers reached his crotch she closed her hand around his burgeoning erection. For a moment she held him lightly. Then she closed her hand and cradled his firming shaft.

"This is the first time I've ever bathed with a man," she confessed. "But it just seemed to be too good a chance to miss. Or would you rather dry off and go to bed?"

"What pleasures you, pleasures me," Longarm replied.

"Then let's stay here in the tub for a while. I feel so free and weightless that I'd like to see what lovemaking in a bathtub is like. And I can feel that you're ready now. So am I, just in case you can't feel it the way I can on you."

9

Jeanne did not wait for Longarm to reply. While she was talking, she was parting her thighs and rolling her hips from side to side as she slid the hand holding Longarm's full erection between them. Longarm lifted his hips as she placed him. Then he drove to enter her with one long thrust. Impeded by the water, the lunge was gentler than he'd experienced before.

"Oh, this is wonderful!" Jeanne gasped as Longarm completed his drive.

For a few moments she did not move. Then she raised her thighs higher and clasped her ankles around his hips. Tightening her leg muscles, she pulled him closer to her, trying to achieve a still-deeper penetration. When Longarm began rocking his hips, he found that he was forced by the water's resistance to thrust more deliberately than was his custom.

If Jeanne minded his slower rhythm, she did not object. She sighed with pleasure as he settled down to a steady rhythmic stroking. Turning up her face, she offered Longarm her lips. Without breaking the regularity of his thrusts, he bent his head to the kiss.

Spurred by their exchange of lip and tongue caresses, Longarm tried to speed the tempo of his drives, but was hampered by the water. Jeanne was twisting her hips now, and he could feel her body beginning to quiver in his arms. He sensed that her time was arriving, and tried to thrust with his usual quick deep lunges, but the water hampered his efforts.

Locking his arms around Jeanne's back, Longarm lifted her without breaking their bond of flesh. He carried Jeanne with him as he stepped from the bathtub and took the two or three long steps necessary to reach the bed. Still buried within her, he dropped to the bed, carrying

Jeanne with him as he fell, and thrusting even deeper as they landed.

Jeanne gasped. Then she began twisting her hips and raising them in rhythm with Longarm's lunges. No longer impeded by the water, he drove faster now. Stroke followed stroke, and as the moments passed Longarm began stepping up the tempo of his drives.

Jeanne was breathing gustily by this time, her eyes squeezed shut, deep breaths following each of Longarm's deep thrusts. Moments ticked off, seeming to be speeded by her gasps. Once she opened her eyes at the breaking of one of their long-held kisses and whispered hoarsely, "Don't hurry, Longarm. I've never enjoyed anything like this before and I don't want it to end!"

"Don't worry," he assured her. "I ain't in no hurry to rush things myself."

For a few moments, Longarm held himself in Jeanne as deeply as he could penetrate. Then he began stroking again, slowly and deliberately, until Jeanne began to shudder, small shivers rippling through her body. Soon the quivers were shaking her at shorter intervals, while the upheaving twists of her hips matched the tempo of her gasping inhalations. Then the rippling shivers did not stop.

When he felt Jeanne starting to quiver almost constantly, Longarm once more slowed the tempo of his lusty driving. At the end of each deliberate lunge he held himself motionless for a moment or two, buried deeply, waiting for Jeanne's small ecstatic shudders to die away. Then he began stroking again, slowly at first, speeding during the moments when Jeanne's responses matched his own timing. The moment came when her quivering did not stop.

Longarm was as ready as Jeanne, and now he did not hold back. He speeded up, forcing himself to delay until Jeanne's climactic gasps began bursting from her throat in a steady low-pitched tone and his own body began to match the quivering of hers. Now Longarm pounded in short deep thrusts that brought the rising and falling cries of ecstastic completion from Jeanne's throat. As she shuddered into the final moments of her climax, Longarm released his control and jetted as he joined her in the completion of their prolonged embrace.

# Chapter 2

"I hate to see you leave, even if I know you'll only be gone a little while," Jeanne said.

"Whatever Billy Vail wants to tell me ought not take more'n a few minutes," Longarm assured her. He was fully dressed, standing beside the bed where Jeanne lay stretched out, covered by a sheet. Sitting down in a chair that faced her, he began levering his feet into his boots as he went on. "I'll maybe be gone an hour, but likely it won't even be that long."

"You know I'd rather have you in bed with me than off doing something else, even if I understand that whatever's taking you away is something important to you."

"It sure is, from what little bit Billy Vail told me. But after I finish talking with him there won't be nothing else to keep me away. You and me'll have the rest of tonight and the better part of tomorrow morning to ourselves, before it'll be time for you to take your train."

"Don't remind me that we have such a short time left

to be together," Jeanne replied with a little grimace of distaste. "At least, not now."

"We'll just have to make do with what we got," he said. "Now, it ain't too far from the hotel here to the office, and thinking about you waiting for me is sure going to keep me in a hurry to get back."

Longarm stood up and stamped his feet, settling them properly into his boots. He stepped to the bed and bent down for Jeanne's good-bye kiss. As she sat up to meet his lips the sheet slid away, and Longarm resisted the temptation to carry his lips down to the globes of her perfect breasts. He stood up quickly, hurried to the door, and started down the carpeted corridor to the stairs.

At this hour of the night the hotel lobby was deserted except for a sleepy-eyed night clerk. The clerk was leaning on the registration desk with his head propped up on one arm, his eyes half-closed. If he noticed Longarm passing through the lobby he gave no indication of it.

Outside in the chilly near-midnight air, Denver slept. Now and then a hansom cab rumbled past. Here and there a light still showed in a shopwindow, and bright strips glowed at the tops and bottoms of the swinging doors of saloons along the street. Longarm turned off Fourteenth Street into Colfax. The Federal Building was a tall dark shape against the moonless starry sky. No lights showed in any of its windows.

Longarm frowned as he glanced up the side of the building and saw that like all those around it the windows of the U.S. marshal's offices were dark. "Now, it ain't like Billy to be late," he muttered under his breath. "Especially when he knows I got other fish to fry tonight. But I guess all I can do is wait for him."

A few more steps took him past the Federal Building's

corner, and he rounded it without breaking his stride. Then he smiled, for even in the dim light cast by the street lamp halfway down the block he recognized the familiar chunky figure of the chief marshal. Vail was pacing up and down in front of the building. When he caught sight of Longarm he stopped at the steps leading up to the entrance doors.

"I was about to give up on you," he said when Longarm got within speaking distance. "I've been waiting for you—"

"Maybe as long as three or four minutes, Billy?" Longarm asked. "I sure ain't late enough to've put you out much."

Even in the dimness Longarm could see Vail's lips curling in a smile. Then the chief marshal said, "I guess I've got to agree with you, Long. I don't suppose I've waited as long as it seemed to be."

"Well, now that I'm here, let's go on up to the office and get down to business," Longarm suggested. "I'd a heap rather be with that little lady who's waiting for me to get back to the hotel than I would with you."

While they were talking they'd mounted the steps to the Federal Building's imposing entrance doors, which were ornamented with deep-relief figures of twin spread-winged American eagles. Vail took out his keyring and selected the key as they stepped up to the wide doors. He opened one of the doors and stood aside, gesturing for Longarm to go in first. Then he followed Longarm in and bent to find the keyhole. For some reason, the locking bolt refused to turn.

"Damn it!" Vail snapped as he struggled to shift the position of the key in the keyhole. "This is the contrariest lock I've ever run into! The trouble is, the building custodian has always unlocked the doors before I get here, and he's the one who locks them when all the offices have closed in the evening."

"You want me to take a shot at turning that key, Billy?" Longarm asked. "Maybe I can get it to snap closed."

"Well, I'm sure not getting anywhere," Vail replied. "Go ahead and see if you can turn the damned key."

Longarm stepped up to the door and for a moment wriggled the big key back and forth and from side to side. Then he tried turning it, and at one point in his efforts pulled the door open as he tried to turn the key, but his attempts were no more successful than Vail's had been.

"It's sure a stubborn booger, all right," he said. "And you can see I ain't having no better luck than you did."

Vail did not reply at once, then he said, "We'll only be staying in the office a few minutes. Let's just leave the damned door unlocked and go on upstairs, Long. All we're doing now is wasting time, and I know you want to get back to your lady at the hotel as soon as you can. There won't be anyone trying to get into the office at this time of the night."

"Whatever you say, Billy," Longarm told him. "And the sooner I get back to the hotel, the better I'll feel."

Closing the door, he followed Vail to the staircase. By this time the eyes of both men had become accustomed to the darkness, and though Vail struck a match as they navigated the turns in the stairs, they had no difficulty ascending them, even in the gloom.

They turned down the corridor to the marshal's office, and this time Vail's key did the job for which it was designed. The office door opened, and they entered. A

16

feeble trickle of starshine came through the windows of the big main room. It was bright enough to enable them to find their way easily through the zigzag course between the desks and chairs that occupied the chamber. Longarm followed Vail into the chief marshal's private office. Vail struck a match and touched it to the wick of the Argand lamp that stood on his desk. The lamp flickered for a moment, then settled down to a warm yellow glow.

Settling into his chair behind the desk, Vail opened its center drawer. Longarm pulled a chair up to the desk's corner as Vail took a small thin packet of folded papers from the drawer and dropped it on the desktop. Longarm made no effort to pick up the papers, but looked at them, frowning.

"You mean I got to read a lot of stuff like that?" he asked.

"It'll only take you a minute or so to go through those messages," the chief marshal replied. "And I'm giving them to you to read so you can be thinking about the new case you'll be leaving on as soon as you can fresh-pack your saddlebags."

"Now, wait a minute, Billy!" Longarm protested. "I been traveling four days to get back to Denver, and here you go putting me on a new case before I've had a chance to get my laundry done and sleep a night or two in my own bed instead of on the damn hard ground!"

"I know that," Vail replied. "But you'll see that this case is . . ." He stopped short and raised his hand, his palm toward Longarm, who recognized the familiar signal to be silent.

In the total stillness of the private office, the scraping of feet on the floor of the big outer room sounded loud indeed. Longarm and Vail exchanged glances. Vail nodded and gestured toward the door. The chair Longarm had settled into was on one side of the big desk that dominated the room. He rose quickly, and saw that Vail was getting to his feet. Moving silently and not speaking, the two men angled to the door leading to the outer office.

By long habit, Vail had closed the door only halfway. Longarm reached it first and pressed his head against the crack between door and jamb. Through the narrow slit he could see the moving form of a man, but the intruder's features were hidden by the shadows of the big entry room.

Turning back to Vail, he whispered, "Somebody's followed us in here, but I can't see whoever it is plain enough to get much of an idea what he looks like."

"It can't be anybody from our outfit, or they'd light a lamp," Vail said. His voice was pitched as low as Longarm's. "Give me a minute to blow out my desk light so we won't be giving him a target. Then step over by the wall, there, and yank the door wide open. We'll jump him at the same time."

Longarm nodded and drew his Colt. Vail slid his revolver out of the shoulder holster he favored and pressed himself along the wall at the edge of the door. Longarm was leveling his Colt as he reached for the doornob. Vail nodded. Longarm got a firm grip on the brass knob and yanked the door open.

In the nearly complete blackness of the big outer office Longarm and Vail saw the silhouetted figure of the intruder drop to the floor. The man moved before either of them could get him in their sights. The darkness in the outer office was so intense that they could not see the intruder, but they could hear the scraping and rattling of chair legs he bumped into as he wormed along the floor.

"Watch the door, Long!" Vail exclaimed. "He's trying to get away!"

A shot rang out from the prowling man's revolver, and both Longarm and Vail dropped to the floor. The spurt of red muzzle-blast had lasted long enough to enable them to fix the intruder's position. Longarm's shot in the general direction of the prowler was echoed by a shot from Vail, but the thunking of lead into the office wall told them that they'd both missed.

The scrabbling noise of the intruder's booted feet followed the shots. Then the door from the office into the hallway creaked as the fleeing man reached it. Neither Longarm nor Vail spoke, but both of them jumped up, revolvers ready. They were too late to get a glimpse of the fleeing man, but the creaking of the door into the corridor had given them the clue they needed. Longarm and Vail dashed toward the door.

In the pitch-black hall, they could see even less clearly than they'd been able to in the office. Both Longarm and the chief marshal paused outside the door as they listened, trying to determine the direction in which the intruder was moving. Only a few instants passed before the clatter of booted feet sounded from the stairwell.

"He's getting away down the stairs!" Vail said. "Let's go after him!"

Longarm was already moving toward the staircase. Small high-set windows broke the wall of the stairwell at intervals, and though very little light trickled through them, the darkness was not as deep as it had been in the office. Longarm hurried down the steps, taking them two at a time even in the darkness. He heard Vail's footsteps following his as the chief marshal hurried to catch up, and when he reached the lobby and started toward the outer door Vail was very close behind him.

Stopping at the top of the steps leading to the sidewalk outside, Longarm scanned the deserted street below. Beyond the small circle of brightness cast by the streetlight he saw no sign of movement. He was turning to search the intersecting street when Vail joined him.

"You'd be running to catch up with that fellow if he was anywhere in sight, so I take it that you've lost him," Vail said. "Which way do you suppose he went?"

"Your guess is as good as mine, Billy." Longarm was taking one of his long slim cigars from his pocket as he spoke. He fumbled a match from his pocket, flicked his iron-hard thumb-nail across its head, and drew until the tip of the cigar glowed, then took it from his mouth as he went on. "He had too much of a lead on us. We ain't got a notion which way he turned."

"That might not matter too much," Vail said. "You take Fourteenth, I'll take Colfax. Chances are he's just ducked into the closest doorway for cover. He hasn't had time to move any real distance."

"That makes good sense," Longarm agreed. "That fellow was sure as hell after one of us, and I'd give a pretty penny to find out why and who he is."

"So would I," Vail said. "But if we're going to catch up with him, we'd better be trying to find him instead of talking."

They moved apart now. Vail started toward the Cherry Creek Bridge and Longarm headed for the street corner, in the direction of the Fourteenth Street intersection. In the darkness of the deserted street they lost sight of one another almost at once.

Longarm began zigzagging at once. He crossed the

street from one of the buildings to another, peering into the darkness of the narrow spaces between them, listening as intently as he looked, hoping for a sound that would give him a clue, or for a glimpse of a moving figure. He saw nothing and heard nothing, except for one occasion when he stepped into one of the narrow spaces between two buildings. The menacing growl of a dog followed by a few sharp barks told him that the fugitive would most certainly have backed away from the dark opening as quickly as he did himself.

"You know, old son," Longarm muttered into the darkness, "this here's just going to be another wild-goose chase. There's three or four other ways besides this one that fellow could've taken, and me and Billy can't cover all of 'em fast enough. What you better do at that next corner is to cut on back to Colfax. Chances are by now that Billy's getting the same idea."

Satisfied he'd made the right decision, Longarm turned back at the next corner, heading for the street's angling junction with Colfax. He'd taken only a few steps when even in the darkness and at a distance he recognized Vail's stocky form approaching him. The chief marshal was moving slowly, and Longarm lengthened his stride.

"I see I'm not the only one who got what the little boy shot at," Vail commented as they came within speaking distance.

"You didn't see him either then?"

"Not hair nor hide," Vail replied. "He had too much of a start on us, and it's a pretty good chance that he'd have been able to give us the slip even if it had been daylight."

"Well, you're calling the shots, Billy. What do you figure we better do now?"

"Go back up to the office. You didn't have a chance to look at the file I wanted you to see before that fellow tried to jump us a while ago."

"You're sure you don't want to wait and show it to me in the morning?" Longarm asked.

"I'm sure," Vail replied.

Longarm recognized the no-nonsense tone of Vail's voice and knew that the chief marshal was not going to change his mind.

Vail went on. "If you can get your mind off that little lady waiting for you at the hotel and go over the file tonight, you might get some stray notion about it that'll save us time in the morning. Besides, I didn't lock the office door when we took out after that fellow."

"Let's step along and get busy then," Longarm said. "The sooner I get through going over it, the better."

Neither Longarm nor Vail had anything more to say while they walked the short distance back to the Federal Building. As they mounted the steps to the doorway, Vail said suddenly, "I feel like a fool, Long. Do you realize that we left the front door of this building open?"

"I didn't give it a thought, Billy. You and me both was in a sorta hurry when we left. But at this time of night, I'd say you don't need to worry because you didn't lock up proper."

"Maybe not, but it makes me feel like a fool, not thinking about it."

"When you're in the middle of a shooting scrape, you ain't got time to think about much except the fellow that's trying to cut you down, Billy. Leastways, that's how I feel."

"I suppose you're right."

They'd reached the door now, and Vail grasped the ornate bronze handle to pull it open. As though his move had been a signal, two quick shots rang out from the dark lobby. The red muzzle-blasts that accompanied them gave both Longarm and Vail a fleeting glimpse of a shadowed figure on the bottom step of the wide stairway inside.

Longarm was quicker to draw than Vail. His answering shot came a fraction of a second before Vail's gun sounded. The man on the stairway triggered off another shot as his fingers cramped in his death throes.

During the fleeting instant when the muzzle-blasts of their two weapons flared, Longarm and Vail had gotten another fleeting glimpse of the man who'd tried to cut them down. He was standing at the bottom of the wide stairway, his revolver sagging as his gun hand fell. In the swift return of darkness, they heard his weapon clatter as it hit the floor.

Neither Longarm nor Vail spoke for a moment. Then Longarm said, "That son of a bitch made fools outta both of us, Billy. He didn't run away at all when we took out after him. He just found a dark place a ways down the hall from the office and holed up, because he figured we'd be coming back right soon."

"Yes, the same thought occurred to me," Vail said. "But he didn't count on us being able to draw damned near as fast as he could pull the trigger."

"Well, we got him," Longarm said. "Now let's see if we can figure out who he is."

Groping their way in the darkness, Longarm and Vail managed to lift the dead man and carry him up the stairs. In the spacious outer room of the marshal's office, they lighted the lamps that stood on the desks, and for the first time got a clear look at the would-be assassins.

There was only one feature of his otherwise common-place face that set it apart from others. A half inch or so above his jawline a long jagged scar, unquestionably the mark of a knife duel somewhere in the dead man's past, ran from the lobe of his left ear along his lower cheek and ended at his chin.

Aside from the scar, the dead killer's face might have been that of a hundred other wanted men whose descriptions were given on the wanted circulars in the files of sheriffs and marshals' offices throughout the West.

"I can't for the life of me recall a killer that's carrying around a scar like that one," Longarm observed after he and Vail had finished their examination.

"Neither can I," Vail said. "And I suppose my memory's about the same as yours."

"Maybe the Denver police file might have him in their wanted circulars," Longarm suggested. "Or maybe we'll find something in his pockets. We still ain't turned them out yet."

He and Vail knelt beside the body and set to work emptying the dead man's pockets. When they deposited their findings on the nearest desk and began going through them, the results were scanty and not at all helpful. Their search had yielded a small handful of coins, mixed gold and silver, totaling a bit more than sixty dollars. It had also produced a wadded bandanna kerchief, a pocketknife, a small handful of matches, and three crushed cigars.

"We're not any further along than we were when we started going through his pockets," Vail observed, looking down at the small scattered array on the desktop. "And we know we didn't miss anything."

Longarm had just put a cigar in his mouth and was

striking a match with his thumbnail. The match flared as Vail finished speaking. Instead of touching the match flame to his cigar, Longarm blew it out. Taking the cigar from his lips, he said, "Hold on, Billy! I just thought about something that maybe we've missed, and it won't take but a minute to find out if I'm wrong or right!"

# Chapter 3

"What kind of something are you talking about?" Vail asked. "You lost me just now."

"It's something that just struck me," Longarm replied. "Take a look at that fellow's belt."

Frowning, Vail turned to glance at the recumbent form of the would-be assassin. "I don't see . . ." he began. Then he nodded and fell silent while the small frown of discouragement that had formed on his face vanished.

Longarm had not waited for Vail to reply to his remark. Even before he'd finished speaking he'd dropped to a knee beside the corpse. Bending forward, he started to unbuckle the wide thick leather belt girding the dead man's waist. The very bulk of the belt as he freed it and pulled it away from the dead man's limp, leaden weight told Longarm that his sudden hunch had been right.

"Both of us oughta been smart enough spot a belt like this when we were going through that dead man's pockets," Longarm remarked as he rose to his feet. "There's something wrong with anybody that don't carry around some backup cash and maybe a private letter or papers of some sort."

"I'll admit thinking that he sure was traveling light when we didn't get more than we did out of his pockets," Vail said. "It just didn't come to mind that he might've had some sort of secret cache."

"Sure." Longarm turned the belt over in his hand and revealed the long slit in the thin Morocco leather of its hidden inner lining. Now that the belt's bulk was visible, they saw it was almost the thickness of a man's finger.

Probing into the slit, Longarm pulled out a packet of currency, the bills folded lengthwise to fit into the hidden space. Handing the money to Vail, Longarm returned his attention to the belt. Its secret compartment yielded another packet of currency as thick as the first, then two more stacks of bills as Longarm continued his exploration.

Scattered along the length of the belt's slit he found a number of gold pieces, ten- and twenty-dollar coins and a few fives. As Longarm retrieved them he placed them on the desk for Vail to stack. His final find was an envelope. It was thin, and had been folded lengthwise. A section of the envelope's front had been torn away, obviously to conceal the name and address of the man to whom it had been sent. However, the rubber-stamped postmark across the upper edge remained untouched.

Longarm passed the envelope to Vail, who glanced at the cancellation mark and said, "Whoever sent this mailed it about three weeks ago from Phoenix, that new town down in Arizona Territory, the one that's supposed to be getting big so fast."

"I already noticed that, Billy. I'm curious about what's inside of it."

Vail was already opening the envelope's flap and taking out the single sheet of paper the battered envelope contained. He scanned it in one quick glance and held it out to Longarm. The letter had no date, no salutation, no signature. Longarm read it aloud:

"Here's your pay for getting rid of Long. You know what will happen to you if you don't earn it."

Looking up from the letter, Longarm commented, "I'd say from this that somebody's holding a pretty strong grudge against me, Billy. That's a big pot of cash we dug outta that belt."

Vail glanced at the stack of currency on the desk and said, "I didn't take time to count it, but my guess is it'll tally up to about two thousand dollars."

"Maybe I oughta feel flattered that somebody'd pay all that much to get shed of me, but I don't. It just makes me mad."

"It's not anything new," Vail reminded him. "We've both had hired gunmen after us, Long."

"Oh, sure," Longarm agreed. "But I ain't put in much time lately in Arizona Territory. It's been most of a year since I had a case there. I guess when I was in them parts the last time, I stepped on somebody's sore toes hard enough to make 'em want to kill me."

"You ought to remember a name or two from that case," Vail suggested.

"Well, I been doing a mite of thinking while we been talking, but I sure can't put a name to whoever wrote this. Not yet, anyways. Of course, it might come to me later on."

"Whoever it was must be pretty well-heeled." Vail frowned thoughtfully. "Something like this does have a pretty sobering effect on a man. I'd say that what you need is a little bit more time to think. You're still officially off duty until you report in to the clerk. Maybe the best thing you can do is just go about your unfinished business and show up here whenever you feel like it."

Longarm studied Vail's face for a moment before replying. The chief marshal's expressionless countenance was as guileless as he'd seen it during their poker games. "Then, I don't guess you'd mind if I didn't report in till afternoon?"

"You heard what I just said," Vail replied. "And if it'll ease your conscience, I'll tell you why I said it."

"I think I got a pretty good hunch, but go on."

"As soon as you leave," Vail continued, "I intend to hail a hack and go down to police headquarters to report why this dead man's been shot. They get a lot of wanted flyers that we don't see, outlaws who aren't on our federal lists. His picture might be on one of them, but we won't know for sure until pretty late in the day."

"Your figuring makes good sense, Billy," Longarm said. "So that being the case, I'll bid you good night and go about my own affairs till I report in."

In the soft light that trickled into the room from the open bathroom door, Longarm saw Jeanne sit up in bed when he turned the key in the corridor door to lock it behind him. The sheet that covered her had slipped away when she raised herself from the mattress, and the sight of her generously bulging rose-tipped breasts and glowing white skin drew his eyes as a powerful magnet draws metal shavings.

"I thought you never were coming back," Jeanne told Longarm as he turned toward her.

"Now, you know I wouldn't stay away from you a minute more than I had to," Longarm assured her while he unbuckled his gunbelt and began shedding his clothes. "But I run into a mite of trouble that I wasn't figuring on."

"I hope it wasn't anything serious."

"Oh, it was just swapping a few shots with a backshooter that tried to cut down me and Billy Vail." Longarm was levering out of his boots.

Jeanne's eyebrows shot up and her brow furrowed as she asked, "You mean you had a gunfight?"

"That brush we had didn't last long enough to call it a fight. Like I said, we just swapped shots. The fellow that started the ruckus dodged too slow." By this time Longarm had kicked away his trousers and was pulling off his shirt. He went on. "He's stretched out back in the Federal Building, about as dead as anybody can be."

"And neither you or Marshal Vail was hurt?"

"Oh, that outlaw wasn't much of a gunhand. Billy's fine, and I guess with me standing here buck naked like I am you can see that I ain't bleeding no place."

"And you won't have to leave me so soon, the way you did before, to go back to your job?"

"I don't aim to set foot in that office till I've seen your train pull out," Longarm assured her. He had not stopped undressing while they talked, and he now had on nothing but his undersuit.

"And that's going to be sooner than either one of us likes to think about," Jeanne said. "So why are we wasting our time talking?"

As she spoke, Jeanne kicked away the sheet that covered her and levered herself off the bed. Two short steps took her to where Longarm was standing. She helped him strip off his thin summer underwear, and as the flimsy garment fell to the floor she pressed her body to him and whispered, "Carry me to bed the way you did before. I've never had such a thrill as you gave me then."

Longarm slid his big strong hands into her armpits and raised her. Jeanne found his erection and placed him, then clasped her thighs around his waist and tightened them to pull him into her. When Longarm felt the beginning pressure of her legs he thrust, and she gasped happily as he went into her.

Two short shuffling steps took them to the bed. He fulfilled Jeanne's request, falling forward, landing on top of her, and feeling himself go even deeper as the her back struck the mattress. Jeanne trilled a throaty cry of pleasure. Longarm began stroking, and she matched his rhythm.

Time stopped in the room that was their small and short-lived world as they explored the gamut of earthly delights. They prolonged their caresses until the sun's rays striking the window shade warned them of the passage of time. Jeanne lifted herself on an elbow and looked down at Longarm.

"Look," she said, gesturing toward the windows. "Judging by the angle of the sunlight, it must be close to noon."

"I know," he replied. "And you got a train to catch before too long."

"You know I wouldn't be leaving unless I had to," she said. "But my responsibility's just as demanding as yours. Both of us understand that. Let's just make the best of it and get on with what we have to do."

• • •

Though he tapped at the half-opened door of Vail's office, Longarm did not wait for the chief marshal's nod of invitation before stepping inside. Vail brushed aside part of the mass of papers that littered his desk as Longarm dropped into his favorite red-upholstered chair.

"I take it that you've got all your personal business settled?" Vail asked.

"Finished and done, Billy. And I appreciate . . ."

Longarm stopped short as Vail waved him to silence. Then Vail said, "Don't be so quick about thanking me. I know you've just gotten back from a case that meant a lot of traveling, and I'd like to say you're going to be able to have a few cases close to Denver. By now, you know that things have a habit of not working out the way you want them to."

"Meaning you're figuring to send me to Arizona Territory?"

"As much for your own good as for getting this case closed," Vail replied.

"Now, Billy, what you're saying about it being for my own good don't exactly make sense," Longarm protested. "That fellow somebody sent here to kill me's dead."

"Suppose the man who sent him sent another killer as well," Vail suggested. "Just on the chance that you might beat the first one to the draw."

"Ain't that sorta stretching it a mite, Billy?"

"If you'll stop and think a minute, you'll see that I don't think so," Vail said soberly. "I want you to stay alive and be the one who winds this case up. Damn it, Long, I'm not going sit on my ass and do nothing when somebody sends a hired killer after one of my deputies! I'm not sending you just because you were that gunman's target. You're going after the son of a bitch because you're the best man I've got in this office and I figure I can count on you finding him!"

"Well, I guess I got to take that as a compliment, Billy," Longarm said. "While I was coming up here from the depot, I was thinking about that hired gunman coming all this way to put me down, and I got to admit, I'm more'n a little bit mad myself."

"Oh, I took that into consideration when I decided to give you the case." Vail smiled, not a whole-hearted grin, but a quick twitch of his lips.

"There's just one thing bothers me," Longarm said. "How in tunket are we going to find out who I'm going after when I get to Arizona Territory?"

"That's been bothering me too," Vail admitted. "But I think I've come up with an idea."

"Trot it out then. Let's lay it down on your desk and get a good look at it."

"Here's what I'm thinking about," Vail went on. "I was sitting here staring at that envelope the note we found on the gunhand was in."

"There wasn't a hell of a lot to stare at as I recall," Longarm observed.

Vail dug into the scattered heap of papers that he'd pushed aside when Longarm entered. He finally found the envelope that they'd taken from the dead man's money belt and handed it across his desk to Longarm.

"If you'll look at that real close," Vail said, "you'll see it's been folded the long way so it'd fit his belt, and it's just as flat as a flapjack."

"Sure," Longarm said. "We saw that when I took it outta that belt he'd hid it in."

34

"That's right," the chief marshal said. "And all of a sudden it hit me that there wouldn't've been room in that envelope to hold all the money we took out of his belt."

"Now that you mention it, those bills weren't in one big wad. They were in a whole bunch of little chunks, spread all along the belt. And there was a pretty good-sized bunch of hard money, but it was all loose."

"Nobody could've squeezed all the money into that one envelope," Vail noted. "As soon as I'd realized that, the bell rang, and I knew besides that sheet of paper with the note on it, there must've been a check or draft or some kind of order made out to a bank here in Denver to pay the killer."

"And that check'd have his real name on it," Longarm added quickly. "Damned if you ain't hit it, Billy! Now all we got to do is go around to all the banks in Denver till we find one that's got a big draft from a bank in Arizona Territory lately."

"Just exactly what I was driving at," Vail said.

"It ought not to be too big of a job. How many banks are there here in Denver now? Something like five or six, as I recall."

"More like seven or eight," Vail said. "I think eight's the right number now, so it'd likely to take a little bit of time to run down the one we're after."

"And I reckon I'm the one that's going to be doing the running?" Longarm asked.

"It's your case," Vail reminded him. "And there sure isn't any use in you starting for Arizona Territory until we've got something solid to go on."

"By solid you mean after I find out whose name was on that draft?"

"Exactly," Vail said. "All of the banks here would keep a record of the checks or drafts they've cashed for banks outside of Denver. And from reading that letter I'm dead sure that gunhand got all the money we found on him by cashing a draft."

"Everything you've said sounds real reasonable," Longarm told Vail. "That draft would have been for a pretty good-sized amount of money, so any bank would keep a record of the name of the man who wrote it and the name of the one who cashed it."

Glancing at his wall clock, Vail went on. "There's a good part of the day left for you to work, so you might as well start now. All the banks stay open until six, and before the day's out maybe you'll be lucky enough to stumble onto the one we're looking for."

"It'd help if I know the name of that dead man too, the one that give us such a bad time last night," Longarm suggested. "He ain't from nowhere close around here, I'll lay a money bet on that."

"I've already got the city police trying to find out who he is," Vail told him. "Sergeant Mulcahy at the central station is going over their wanted notices right now. I ought to hear from him before too long."

"I'll start working the banks then," Longarm said as he stood up. "I don't reckon I'll get to all of 'em before six o'clock, but if I put in the rest of the day I oughta be able to get around to three, maybe four. I got a real strong hankering to find out who it is that's mad enough at me to try and have me put outta the way."

•

"You understand, Marshal Long, that in a bank of this size we handle hundreds of checks every day, and they come from all parts of the country, from New York to San

Francisco," the vice-president of the Colorado National Bank said. "We'll be closing in less than an hour, and I'm afraid it would take a great deal more time than that to find the information you're asking for."

"Well, now, Mr. Saunders," Longarm replied, his voice quietly thoughtful, "it seems like I recall that when the Wild Bunch came outta the Hole in the Wall a while back and started holding up banks all around Denver, it didn't take a lot of time for our marshals to stand guard here in your bank, and just because you were afraid you'd be held up too."

For a moment the banker was silent, then he smiled and said, "You've made your point very well, Marshal Long. I'll have a clerk start going over our check-clearance lists right away. Would you care to wait and see if we did indeed handle the check you're interested in tracing?"

"You got any idea how much time it'll take?" Longarm asked.

"Not more than a quarter of an hour," Saunders assured him. "We cross-index all the checks from outside Denver by the name of the payee and date and city of origin."

"I'll wait, then," Longarm said. "If you'll just show me someplace where I'll be outta your way . . ."

"Oh, I'll take you to our preferred-client waiting room," the banker said. "I'm sure you'll find it quite comfortable."

Leading the way along a carpeted corridor, Saunders stopped at one of the doors and swung it open. He gestured for Longarm to enter. The room was furnished with deep-seated leather-upholstered lounge chairs, and was dominated by a gleamingly polished round mahogany table that held a large silver tray. On it were bottles of

37

choice whiskeys and brandies. Glasses were stacked on a second and smaller tray.

"Please pour yourself a drink while you wait," the banker said. "I'll get one of our clerks busy at once."

Longarm waited until Saunders had closed the door behind him before moving to the table. Under his breath he muttered, "Well, now. You got a chance to see how rich folks live. And even act like you're rich for a little while."

His inspection of the liquor bottles showed that Tom Moore's Maryland Rye was not among them. There was a bottle of rye, however, an ornate bottle bearing the legend "Gibson's Choice Rye Whiskey." Longarm muttered to himself, "This here's the real expensive stuff. And seeing that there ain't no barkeep to pour and then get higher prices for choice rye, you better put away a sip while you got the chance."

Picking up a glass from the tray, he poured a generous tot of the liquor into it. He sipped approvingly, then stepped to one of the easy chairs and settled into it before lighting a fresh cigar.

"Old son," Longarm said softly as he exhaled a cloud of blue-gray smoke, "you might have to wait a while before that bank fellow gets back, but you got to give him credit. Maybe he'll keep you waiting for a spell, but this is one time you can wait and be comfortable all at once."

# Chapter 4

Longarm leaned back in the easy chair and stretched his booted feet straight out in front of him. Each sip of the mellow but biting rye whiskey that he swallowed between puffs of his stogie went down smoothly, leaving an authoritative aftertaste. He'd emptied the glass and refilled it once during the quarter hour or so following Saunders's departure, and was standing beside the table pouring still another glassful when the door opened and the banker reappeared.

"We're both in luck, Marshal Long," Saunders said. "We handle very few bank checks from Arizona Territory, and my clerk had no trouble at all finding the entry you're interested in."

"You mean to say you've already dug up what I was after?" Longarm asked, trying not to sound too surprised.

"I'm sure we have," Saunders replied. "The check you questioned me about was the only one from an Arizona Territory bank that's passed through our books during the current month."

"It'd just about have to be the right one then," Longarm agreed.

"Oh, I'm positive that it is," the banker assured him. He raised his hand to show Longarm a slip of paper. "My clerk jotted down these details. You'll understand that we've already mailed the check itself to the bank where the account's on deposit. That's our standard procedure, but if you should need to introduce the original check as evidence in a criminal trial, it can be subpoenaed from the issuing bank."

"We ain't got to the point of trying a case in court yet," Longarm said. "If it comes down to that, and we need to show it, I'll keep what you said in mind."

"Of course," Saunders replied. He glanced at the slip of paper. "The check was issued in the amount of two thousand dollars. It was drawn on the Security Bank of Arizona Territory, located in Phoenix, against the account of a company named Territorial Enterprises, a corporation. We made out the signature of the payer to be Redford Trent. The payee's name was Frank Smith. It appeared in a different style of handwriting in the endorsement on the back of the check. Our teller also made a memorandum that there was a note jotted in the lower right-hand corner of the check which seems to be in the same handwriting as the other entries by Trent. The memorandum was very brief. It was only two words. 'Services rendered.' "

"You folks keep a pretty good account of the money you take in and pay out, I see," Longarm said. "Now, I might need to know who was at the window where the check was handed in, where it was cashed. I reckon you got that on your paper there too?"

"If you're thinking of asking our teller for a description of the person who cashed it, the payee who signed it as

Frank Smith, I'm afraid I can't help you much on that, Marshal Long," Sanders answered. "Our tellers often move from one window to another during the course of a day. It might be extremely difficult for them to remember details of any patron, except of course those who come in regularly."

"Damned if there ain't too many Smiths in the world!" Longarm snorted. "But with what you've given me, I figure I won't have much trouble finding out the right name of the outlaw that cashed it."

"I hope this isn't going to result in our bank becoming involved in some sort of legal action, Marshal Long," Saunders said soberly. "We try to avoid being brought into criminal trials, even as witnesses."

"Well, now, I can't give you any guarantees, because all that's outta our jurisdiction. We just arrest crooks and leave it to the judges to do the rest in court. Right now, I can't say what's going to happen when things get further along."

"Of course not," Saunders noted. He stopped for a moment, then asked, "Is there any other way we can be of service to you, Marshal Long?"

"I can't see there would be, not right this minute," Longarm answered. "I'll just say thank you for the help and the drink and be on my way."

"I'm very pleased that we could be helpful," the banker replied. "Shall I show you to the door, or—"

"Why, I think I can find my own way easy enough," Longarm said. "It ain't but a few steps."

Outside the bank, Longarm started back to the Federal Building. He was in no hurry, and strolled leisurely along the brick sidewalk. As he entered the marshal's office, the young pink-cheeked clerk sitting at the desk nearest the door gestured toward Vail's private room.

"He's been looking for you this past half hour," the youth said. "And growling because you haven't come in yet."

"Billy likes to growl," Longarm replied. "And I sorta got used to it by now."

Vail saw Longarm approaching the half-open door and called, "What's been holding you up, Long? It's nearly six o'clock."

"I found out all I could about that check, Billy," Longarm replied. "It'll help some, but not all that much more'n the envelope we found in the dead crook's money belt did."

"Suppose you sit down and tell me what you did find out," Vail suggested. He sounded less impatient now, and the frown on his face was dissolving.

Longarm settled into the red-upholstered chair that he favored as he replied, "Well, Billy, about all I really come up with is that a man named Frank Smith's got a hand in this case. Whoever this Frank Smith is, he cashed a check from a bank in Arizona here in Denver."

"And I'd guess the check was for a pretty fancy figure?"

"Two thousand dollars," Longarm nodded.

"And that was all you dug up?"

"Just about. The folks at the bank where the dead man cashed the check have already sent it on to the bank in Arizona. The check was drawn against the account of a company there called Territorial Enterprises. Signed by a man named Redford Trent."

Vail did not speak for a moment, but sat with his eyes half closed. Longarm did not interrupt the chief marshal's thoughts, but sat as silently as Vail.

"I don't suppose there's any way around it," Vail said at last. "Over in Arizona Territory there's a man trying to kill you—or hire somebody to kill you. Maybe this Trent. He missed this time, but chances are that he won't give up. I'm dead sure he'll try again."

"Oh, I sorta feel that way too, Billy," Longarm said. "But this ain't the first time nor even the second one that some outlaw's tried to put me down. Up to now I guess I been lucky."

"That's no guarantee your luck will hold out," Vail reminded him. "We can't afford just to let this pass by, Long."

"So far, I been able to take care of myself pretty good," Longarm protested. "But I don't need to tell you that."

"Of course not," Vail agreed. He was silent again for a moment or two, then went on. "I guess you've heard about a cat having nine lives?"

"Oh, sure. When I was a little tad growing up back in West Virginia, I heard my grandma say that whenever one of us younkers had any sorta accident or got into trouble."

"Did you ever stop to wonder what happened to the cat the tenth time it got in trouble?"

"Now that I come to think of it, I can't say I have, Billy," Longarm answered.

"Well, that's what I'm trying to get across to you," Vail explained. "You've gotten by so far with just a few scratches. But that's no guarantee you'll be lucky or fast enough on the draw the next time whoever's after you sends a hired killer to cut you down."

"You don't have to go no further, Billy," Longarm said. "I can already figure out what you got in mind. When do you want me to leave for Arizona Territory?"

"I haven't said a word yet about sending you any-where," the chief marshal answered.

"Maybe not, but I'd bet a plugged cartwheel against a new pair of boots that's what it's certain to come down to. I figured I might as well come right out and say it myself as wait for you to get around to it."

"Oh, I was getting around to it, all right. Unless you can come up with some better way to find out what's in the mind of this Trent or whoever's behind all this."

"When you ask me so offhand like, Billy, I got to admit I can't," Longarm replied. "But it ain't like I'd be going to someplace where I've never worked a case before."

"This time, you're the case." Vail smiled. "Since we know that this all goes back to Arizona Territory, I'd be neglecting my sworn duty if I didn't send you there to find out why and look into whatever's going on."

"I don't guess you've got a real case out there that we need to look into?"

"Not until that shooting scrape we got into yesterday," Vail said. "You remember Sam Clifton, I suppose?"

"Oh, sure. It was his place I come here to take when he got boosted up to being acting chief over in Arizona Territory."

"Well, the high muckety-mucks in Washington finally confirmed Sam's promotion and he's the chief marshal there now, not just the acting chief anymore. Now, I'm not going to send him a wire that you'll be heading his way. There's too many people that can get their hands on a telegram. What I want you to do is just drop in at his office and say hello for me. And then you tell him what's happened here. I'll guarantee he'll find plenty to keep you busy after he hears about that gunman from his jurisdiction being sent here to cut you down."

"Which means I'll be leaving pretty soon for Arizona Territory?" Longarm asked.

"That means tomorrow," Vail replied. "I'll tell the clerk to get your travel orders and your cash allotment ready. I can't see that there's any reason to waste time."

"For once I ain't going to put up any argument, Billy," Longarm said quickly. "All I got to do after I get my travel vouchers is pick up my rifle and my necessary bag. Then I'll be on the next train heading south."

Longarm had been watching the barren rocky soil from his window on the train since its departure from Flagstaff almost two hours earlier. The tracks did not run straight for any great distance, but wound in long curves that were necessary to avoid bridging the canyons that sliced through the low humps of light brownish-yellow soil, which were the only consistent features of the seemingly endless stretches of virtually barren land.

Usually the landscape was devoid of vegetation. Now and again he saw a scattering of thin-branched cholla cactus or a stretching carpet of red-flowered cow's-tongue cactus. Once in a while a cluster of big-barrel cactus was visible. For the most part, however, the rock-strewn soil, sun-bleached to a light tan and lacking any features other than a scattering of stones, stretched out in monotony.

When the train began to slow down, the voice of the conductor sounded from the rear of the coach. Longarm turned to look at the railroad man as well as to listen.

"Rail-end ahead," the conductor raised his voice to announce. "There's a corral where you can rent a horse or a mule, and you can get whatever valises or parcels you checked in the baggage coach. Just make sure you claim your luggage before the train starts back, because anything you might miss, we'll just have to carry all the way back to Flagstaff."

"How far are we going to be from anyplace?" one of the men in the coach called.

"Where we'll stop at the railhead, we'll only be about six miles from Ash Fork," the conductor replied. "That's where you'll get on the connecting train west. But if you're heading south to Phoenix or Tucson, you'll have to go another ten miles or so on horseback to get to the railhead of the line we're pushing up this way from Prescott."

"And where are we supposed to get the horses in this damn bare desert country?" another asked.

"There'll be plenty of horses and saddle gear for you at a corral where the rails end, and there's no charge for them," the conductor explained. "It's the best we can do to get you where you're going."

"All I can say is, this is a hell of a way to run a railroad!" the first man snorted.

Longarm raised his voice and called, "Now, these men running the train ain't a bit to blame for what we got to do! And there ain't nothing we can do to change things, so we might as well start moving."

Slowly, the grumblings died away and the passengers began pushing toward the vestibule. Though the coach had not been crowded, it had been almost full. Most of the passengers were men, but at the end of the waiting line, in front of Longarm, there were two women. Both were pushing to the age of full maturity.

Longarm had noticed them before, for on several occasions one or another of the male passengers had stopped at the seat the women had occupied at the end of the coach. Each of the men who stopped had tried to begin a conversation, but the women had ignored their efforts.

Both women carried bulging suitcases which they were trying to manage as they shuffled along at the end of the otherwise all-masculine line moving slowly toward the end of the coach. Though Longarm had glanced in their direction a time or two, he'd paid no more attention to them than he had to the other passengers. Now he could see that they were having trouble with their luggage in the suddenly crowded aisle of the coach where the passengers were moving toward the vestibule. On impulse he stepped up to them.

"If you ladies don't mind me butting in, I'd be glad to carry those valises for you," he said. "It looks to me like they're pretty heavy."

"That's quite all right," one said. "We can look after our own bags."

"Oh, I ain't saying you can't," Longarm went on. By looking from one to the other he managed to address both of them at the same time. "My name's Custis Long, and I'm a deputy United States marshal. That ain't neither here nor there, but I want you to know I ain't just some jackleg trying to get acquainted. Now, I put all my gear in the baggage car for the trip, and it'll be waiting for me to pick up any time before the train heads back. But I'd bet I'm a mite stronger than both of you together, and right now I got two free hands that'll ease you from carrying them heavy valises."

After the two women exchanged glances, the one who'd spoken earlier nodded. Her companion responded with a nod of her own. The first woman returned her attention to Longarm and said, "That's very kind of you, Marshal Long. We'll just accept your offer. I'll have to admit, these bags are a bit clumsy and heavy."

47

Dropping their valises to the floor of the coach, both women moved a step away from them as Longarm moved up the aisle. He picked up a suitcase in each hand. By this time the last of the other passengers had left the coach. Sidling along behind the two women, Longarm lugged the valises to the vestibule and down the steps to the ground.

"Any place special you want me to put these suitcases?" he asked. "If you need me to move 'em later on, I'll be glad to do it, but right now I need to hurry on down to the baggage coach and get my own gear before the train starts back."

"Why—over by the horse corral, I suppose," one of the pair replied. "If it's not too much to ask you to carry them that far."

"It ain't but a step, ma'am," Longarm assured her. "And I won't be gone but a minute."

Longarm's minute stretched to much more than that. At the baggage coach he was forced to wait while the two handlers unloaded bags of tie-plates and kegs of spikes into a wagon. His wait was prolonged still further when a quick search for his rifle and necessary bag revealed that they'd been covered by dead freight moved off the rail-laying materials.

By the time he started walking back, carrying his rifle and bag, the whistle announcing the train's departure was blowing. Longarm barely glanced up as the string of cars began moving away on the return trip to Flagstaff. When he reached the corral the two women he'd befriended were standing beside their luggage, worried looks on their faces.

"I'm afraid we're in trouble," one of them said. She gestured toward the corral. Only one horse remained in

48

it now, and the backs of the train's passengers were fast disappearing around a bend in the trail ahead.

"We tried to go in the corral and get horses, but there was such a crowd around the gate that we couldn't break through," the other added. "Now there's only that one horse left, and it certainly can't carry three of us."

"There ain't much doubt about that," Longarm admitted. "But where's the fellow that was in charge of this place?"

"Why, he rode off with the others, while you were up getting your gear," one of them replied.

"You mean he just left without a by-your-leave? And didn't try to help you at all?" Longarm asked.

"He just said he had to lead the men who'd gotten horses as far as the place where the trail splits, because it's hard to find and he didn't want the ones going to Ash Fork to go to Prescott by mistake. Then he told us that we'd have to wait until the passengers coming from Prescott and Ash Fork brought the horses back. That won't be until late tomorrow, and we'll miss making our connection with the westbound train."

"It leaves at noon tomorrow," the other young woman volunteered. "Then there won't be another one for two days."

"I got to admit, it seems like us three sure got what the little boy shot at," Longarm said slowly, his eyes searching the corral and the jerry-built sheds beyond it. "Seems like the railroads are getting worse every day, and they . . ." He stopped short and stepped to one side, his eyes fixed on the area beyond the sheds. Then he turned to the two women. "You ladies just wait here a minute, if you don't mind. It might be we can get started sooner'n we figured."

Circling the corral to the buildings, Longarm went to the ramshackle sheds, and even before he'd rounded the side of the first one he saw that his eyes had not deceived him. A buggy stood behind the shed. Its black paint was cracked and tufts of straw had pushed through torn slits in its seat and back, but its wheels seemed sturdy enough and the shafts seemed intact.

"Well, now," Longarm said aloud. "It ain't such a much, but this old buggy'll carry three at a pinch, and there's the horse we need, right there in the corral."

He'd reached the battered buggy now. Stepping between the shafts, he lifted them and tugged. The buggy started moving as Longarm stepped forward. Pulling the light vehicle was no real challenge to Longarm's strength. An occasional creak sounded while he rolled it out of the shed and up to the corral fence, but it moved easily enough.

Raising his voice, Longarm called to the two women. "Maybe you ladies don't need to worry after all about missing your train connections. This old buggy looks pretty shabby, but if we take it easy and don't try to push too fast, I'm betting it'll get us where we got to go without no trouble at all!"

# Chapter 5

"You ladies might not be any too comfortable in this kind of rig," Longarm said. To the accompaniment of creaks and squeaks he was climbing into the scarred and battered buggy after he'd given the women a hand up. "But you know the old saying about beggars not being choosers."

"Don't worry about us being comfortable," one of the women replied. "There's plenty of room on this seat, and we'll both happy just to be traveling in the direction we need to go."

Settling into his seat, which was slightly too narrow, Longarm slapped the reins on the horse's back and the buggy creaked in a half-dozen new places at once as it started rolling down the narrow trail from the railhead.

"I think we both owe you an apology," the second woman said. "I'm sure you thought we weren't very polite when you introduced yourself to us on the train, Marshal Long. We didn't tell you our names because three or four other men had stopped and fished around,

51

trying to get us to introduce ourselves, and we didn't want to encourage them."

"Oh, I tumbled to that right off," Longarm said. He was dividing his attention between the trail and covertly watching his companions. "And it didn't hurt my feelings a mite."

Longarm had noted from his first glimpse of them that the two young women did not seem to fit into a commonplace mold. When they'd begun talking to him after they'd gotten off the train, it had been obvious to him from the first that they weren't saloon girls. Their behavior and speech did not fit into the patterns of the part-waitresses, part-whores who worked in the bars. Nor did they act like housewives who usually left decisions to their husbands, or like schoolteachers, whose general behavior seemed designed to impress upon others that they were superior beings, a step or two above the commonality.

"My name's Dawn Grey," the young woman who'd spoken first volunteered. She was a short girl, her hair a light-hued brown, with full cheeks and lips. She tended to be a bit chubby, but was far from being like the one of the usual squatty women who displayed a variety of miscellaneous bulges. Dawn's figure was full. She had wide hips and breasts that bulged just a bit too much for her height and stature.

"I'm Retta Boone, Marshal," the other said. She stood a full head taller than her companion, and though she was also full-breasted and wide-hipped, her waist tucked slimly inward and her face tended to be thin. She went on. "Just to save you from asking the question everybody asks, I don't know whether or not my family has any connection with Daniel Boone, the famous frontiersman."

"I'm right pleased to make your acquaintance," Longarm replied. "And I ain't worried about old Dan'l. He's been gone a long time. What I'm thinking about right now is, we got a pretty good-sized trip ahead, and maybe the first thing I better do is tell you that I don't cotton a lot to folks that're stiff and stuffy. I got a sorta nickname that I answer to better'n I do either one of my names. My friends call me Longarm."

"Why, of course!" Dawn smiled. "The long arm of the law! I don't suppose you'd mind if we call you that? And neither of us is very formal. Let's just be ourselves, Dawn and Retta and Longarm."

"That suits me to a tee," he agreed. "Because we got quite a trip up ahead of us, a lot more miles than we can cover in this old buggy during what's left of the day."

"You won't hear either of us complain," Retta said. "We're used to strange trips at odd hours. Both of us are nurses."

"Heading west looking for better jobs?" Longarm asked.

"How did you guess that?" Dawn exclaimed.

"Well, if it don't bother you when I speak my mind, you sure ain't going to be mistaken for saloon girls. Them or nurses are about the only ladies that'd have the gumption to go and travel by themselves to where they can get the best pay. Store clerks generally stay in one town. They ain't apt to move around much."

"Yes, both of us had several jobs that didn't really pay us enough to live on," Retta said. "After a while we found out that nursing was about the best-paying kind of work we could do, so we studied it and passed our courses."

53

"Then we found out that the best pay nurses get is in California," Dawn volunteered. "So we decided to try our luck there."

"We can get twenty dollars a week instead of six, and not work any harder," Retta went on. "Do you blame us for moving?"

"If I could more'n double my pay, I wouldn't waste a minute making up my mind to move," Longarm replied. "But a United States marshal draws down the same pay regardless of where he's working."

"That doesn't seem fair," Dawn observed. "But there are a lot of things in this world that aren't fair to somebody. Now, I don't think it was fair for that man back at the rail-end to take everybody but us to where we need to go to make our train connections for the west."

"Well, it still worked out all right," Longarm said. "We'll get to that other railhead in time for you to get on board your westbound train, and I'll get the one that'll take me where I'm headed for."

"You're not taking the train to the West Coast?" Retta asked.

"Not this trip," he told her. "I've worked a pretty good bunch of cases out there, from the Mexican border on up to the redwood country, but this one I'm on now is here in Arizona Territory."

While they'd been talking, the buggy had been moving steadily forward. Its progress was anything but smooth. There were stretches of soft yellowish-brown soil where the earlier passage of loaded wagons had cut deep ruts, and other stretches where the buggy's wheels bounced along over the rounded tops of closely packed boulders which gave small evidence that any kind of vehicle had ever crossed them before.

On both sides of the wheel ruts the vegetation was sparse. Widely separated stands of cactus dotted the land adjoining the trail, and there were occasional small patches of short yellow-tipped pale green desert grasses, but none of the growth was thick enough to hide the coarse ocher surface of the arid soil.

They rode in virtual silence for the better part of an hour, speaking very little. Now and then their silence was broken when one of the young women pointed out an unusually odd-shaped cactus plant or a rock outcrop that stood out from its arid and virtually featureless surroundings of yellow soil. Ahead of them the dimly marked trail seemed to vanish at the edge of a high wall of stone that jutted above the trail.

Since they'd left the railhead an hour or more earlier, Longarm had been holding the reins only loosely, letting the horse set its own gait. Now he took up the slack, getting ready to check the animal as it entered the sharp curve ahead. The horse veered as it felt the pressure. It began tossing its head from side to side, then started to rear.

Its rearing tightened the reins suddenly. Longarm pulled them in to keep control of the animal. Feeling the unexpected pressure, the horse broke its stride and reared on its hind legs. As it dropped back down, its hoof landed with a loud thunk on a sharply slanting rock outcrop at the edge of the curve. The animal began whinnying with pain. It broke stride and started limping.

Longarm slackened pressure on the leathers, and the horse hobbled around the curve in the road. Seeing that the animal was hurting, Longarm reined in quickly. The horse stopped at once. It was standing on three legs now, its fourth hoof dangling from its upraised leg.

"There's smart horses and fool horses," Longarm commented as he looped the reins around the buggy's whip-socket and swung to the ground. "I got a hunch this one's the kind that's smart enough to stop when it's hurting."

Now the horse was standing on three legs, holding one of its forehooves above the ground. Longarm stepped up to the animal and bent to examine the hoof. He found no rock in the narrow slit of its pastern-cleft, but when he pressed with his horn-hard thumb into the narrow opening, the animal gave another sharp whinny of pain and tried to pull its foot free. Longarm released the hoof and stepped back to the buggy.

"I can figure out now why the fellow that was in charge of things back at the railhead didn't let nobody ride this critter. It's got a real sore hoof."

"Too sore for it to go on?" Dawn asked.

"Well, now, I wouldn't go so far as to say that," Longarm replied. "But it likely won't move easy for a while, not till it stops hurting."

"And how long will that be?" she asked.

"Hard to tell, Dawn. Maybe just a little spell, half an hour or so," he answered. "Maybe not till tomorrow morning."

"But that's likely to make us miss our train!" Retta exclaimed. "We won't get to the railhead in time!"

Longarm shook his head. "Now, that don't rightly follow, Retta. It just might be that if we stop here for a little spell and give the critter a chance to get over being sore, we can make it before that train you're supposed to catch pulls out."

"I don't suppose there's anything we can do about it," Retta said. "So we might as well get out and look around while we're waiting."

Both she and Dawn stepped down from the buggy and came to stand beside Longarm. They looked at the horse's injured hoof. When he raised the animal's leg to show them the source of their problem, Retta slid her fingers into the pastern-cleft and pressed its sore spot. The horse whinnied again, but its snort was not as loud as its earlier snort had been.

"I'm not as well acquainted with horses as I am with people," she told him. "But I have a hunch you're right, Longarm."

"I've worn out more'n one or two of 'em," he told her. "Horses, of course, not people. Most of 'em when I was pushing 'em too hard riding over country pretty much like this. Us and the horse'll all be better off if we wait until morning instead of trying to hurry now."

"Since we're going to stay here, we'd better be looking for a place to sleep," Dawn suggested. She pointed to an area of greenery on a gentle slope of the land a short distance away. "It looks like that little green spot might be better than this rocky ground."

"Likely you're right," Longarm agreed. "And just being on a soft place might help this nag to get over being foot-sore. Suppose you ladies go look. If it suits you, wave at me and I'll lead the nag over there."

Longarm watched the two women as they walked over to the area of greenery. After they'd reached it and looked around for a moment, Dawn turned and waved to Longarm. He looped the reins loosely around the buggy's whip-socket and led the horse toward the patch of greensward.

"We're in luck," she said as Longarm looped the reins around a small boulder at the edge of a room-sized patch of ankle-high green grasses. "This will be a lot better than sleeping on rocks."

"It's lucky we found it," Retta told him.

"We might as well settle in, then," Longarm suggested. "I got some hard-cured sausage in my saddlebags, and a chunk of bread that's likely to be a mite hard to chew by now. That'll tide us over for supper, and we'll just have to wait till we get to the new railhead for breakfast in the morning."

"Neither of us was farsighted enough to bring any food," Dawn confessed. "So we certainly won't have any objections to sharing yours. Both Retta and I carry bedding, because a lot of the time when we're on a case we've got to stay in a strange house overnight, sometimes longer."

"Let's settle in then," Retta suggested. "I've heard that in desert country like this night settles down very quickly."

"It does that," Longarm agreed. "It'll only take me a minute or so to open out my bedroll, so I'll unhitch the nag and tether it where it can graze on that little patch of grass over yonder. And I'll sleep close to it, where I'll be handy in case it gets spooked by something during the night."

Their preparation for the night took very little time, but the sudden darkness of desert country was already settling in by the time they'd finished. The moon was in its dark phase, and the uncountable brilliant stars of the desert night lent a ghostly semi-brightness to the small clearing. After an exchange of good nights, Longarm spread his bedroll, levered out of his boots, and turned in. He was asleep almost before he pulled the blanket over his shoulders. He had no idea how long he'd been sleeping when a muffled grating of feet on the baked soil brought him awake and fully alert. He sat up in his blankets, reaching for the Colt he'd placed beside him as he looked around for the source of the noise. He saw the silhouette of a figure standing beside his bedroll, blocking out the stars, recognized his visitor at once, and even before she spoke lowered his revolver.

"Don't worry, Longarm! It's only me!" Retta said.

Keeping his voice low he asked her, "What's wrong, Retta? Did you hear something that woke you up?"

"I haven't really been asleep," she replied. "I'd doze off, but never could sleep more than a few minutes before I'd wake up and start thinking about you being over here. I don't suppose you'd object if I join you?"

"Why, I wouldn't mind one little bit," he assured her.

Retta slid under the blanket beside him as she said, "I didn't even try to go back to sleep this time, because I got too many ideas. It took me a while to make up my mind to come join you, and here I am."

"You're right welcome too," Longarm assured her.

While he was speaking, Retta's hand was slipping down to Longarm's crotch. She caressed him for a moment through the fabric of his trousers, then slid her fingers under his belt. She fumbled for a moment with the elastic waistband of his underwear, and Longarm felt her exploring his crotch. He was still flaccid, but the stroking and squeezing of Retta's soft hand-caresses quickly started him swelling.

"Thinking about you is what kept me awake this last time I woke up," she whispered. "I just had to find out if you're as much of a man as I think you are."

"Well, now, I'll sure do my best to show you," Longarm said as he slid his arms around her and pressed her to him.

Retta tried to open his fly with her free hand, but its buttons defeated her. Longarm helped her to work them free and Retta liberated him. He was not yet fully erect, but the subtle caresses of her soft questing hands were potent persuaders.

He unbuttoned the neck of her dress, and she shrugged her shoulders and let the garment fall to her waist. In the dim light Longarm could see the dark circles centered in the swell of each white globe of her breasts. He bent to find them with his lips, and rasped their budded tips with his tongue.

A small shudder swept through Retta's body. She reached down to lift her skirt, then pulled Longarm's free hand across the vee of her pubic brush. When he discovered that she had on nothing but her dress, Longarm accepted her unspoken invitation. As he busied his fingers in soft caresses, a fresh wave of shivers shook Retta. She rose to her knees and straddled Longarm's hips. Before he could reach to place her she did so herself, and sank down on his rigid shaft with a happy bubbling sigh.

"Do you mind if I stay on top?" she whispered as the sigh trailed away.

"Whenever a lady asks me that, I always tell her to just go on and do what pleases her the most," Longarm told her.

Retta began rocking her hips. She moved slowly and deliberately at first. After a few minutes she leaned forward to brace her arms on Longarm's shoulders in order to speed her moves and take him deeper. A series of happy sighs bubbled from her lips as she rocked back and forth. Soon she speeded up her rocking movement and started twisting her hips from side to side.

Longarm began thrusting his hips upward in rhythm with Retta's swaying. Her occasional sighs became a series of soft moans and her body began to quiver. Longarm shortened the rhythm of his upthrusts, and Retta's shudders shook her more often.

"I've been without a man too long," she gasped. "And I hope you're ready, because I can't wait much longer."

"You go ahead and pleasure yourself," Longarm said. "But you don't have to be in too big of a hurry. We got all the time we need, and I'm just getting started good."

Retta was panting now, her head thrown back. Longarm grasped her waist in his big hands and lifted her a bit higher to allow her more freedom to move. With her hips now free to swing and swivel, Retta accelerated the tempo of her rocking, twisting movements. She kept up her frantic gyrations for only a moment before Longarm felt her body beginning to quiver.

Small shuddering cries began bursting from her throat, and as they mounted in volume, Retta's trembling increased. Then her hips jerked frantically as a cry of fulfillment bubbled from her throat. Longarm brought up his own hips in a last upward lunge, and held Retta's quivering body impaled while she shuddered to her climax. When her spasms faded to ripples she lurched forward to lie on him full length, until her gasps faded to softly panting inhalations and the ripples that had been shaking her faded and finally ended.

After they'd lain quietly for a few moments, Retta lifted her head and said, "You certainly know how to

61

please a woman, Longarm. I'd like to stay with you a lot longer, but—"

"But your friend's waiting to take her turn," Longarm said, breaking in. "And you're wondering if I got enough spunk left to please her too. Well, Retta, I ain't one to brag, but you tell her to come on over whenever she feels like it."

"So soon?" Retta asked. "Are you sure?"

"Of course I am. It ain't that I want you to go, but I'd be mighty surprised if you and her hadn't fixed up to take turns paying me a little visit."

"We've been underestimating you, Longarm," Retta said. "But you're right. So I'll just kiss you good night and go now. And I hope you can surprise Dawn the way you did me."

When Dawn arrived a few moments later she proved to be a bit more forthright than Retta had been. She looked down at Longarm and said, "You know quite well why I'm here, Longarm. The only thing Retta told me was that I didn't have anything to worry about, and I'm ready for you to show me what she meant."

"Then there ain't no reason for us to waste time," Longarm replied. "Suppose you just stretch out by me here, and I'll do my best to show you what your friend was talking about."

Dawn had dropped to her knees before Longarm finished his invitation, but she did not go further. He'd pulled the fly of his jeans together, but had not buttoned it, and Dawn's questing fingers reached his waist before he could move a hand. She flipped his fly open and her hand darted to grasp him.

"You need some help, Longarm!" she exclaimed when she found that his erection had not yet begun. "And I know you'll enjoy the kind I want to give you."

"I ain't a man that'll say no to a pretty woman," he told her. "Go on and do what pleases you best."

Dawn was already bending forward. Longarm settled back as she engulfed him and her agile tongue began rasping him gently. For the next several minutes she devoted herself to her caresses, and Longarm lay still, his enjoyment mounting. Several minutes ticked away. Then Dawn lifted her head and released him.

"I'm enjoying myself too much to stop," she said. "And if you've got as much steam as I think you have, I'm sure you'll be able to take care of me."

"Do what you feel like doing," Longarm invited her. "I ain't running out of steam, and I don't aim to. Just take your pleasure and don't worry. We can't start moving away from here till daylight, and that's a long time off."

Dawn resumed her attentions to Longarm. He did not try to prolong his pleasure or measure the time that was passing. He let himself enjoy Dawn's caresses to the final moment, and when that moment arrived he lifted her in his strong hands and muscled her above him. Dawn understood his move. Her hand darted down to place him as he lowered her. Longarm rolled to bring himself above her. Then he began driving.

He stepped up the speed of his lunges when she started trembling. Then, as she began crying out in her final ecstastic spasm, he allowed himself the pleasure of release. He twisted to lie down beside Dawn, and when they'd both started to breathe regularly again she said, "If that was meant to be good-bye, I don't think I've ever had a nicer one. But even if I'd like to do it all over from the beginning, I don't guess we'd better."

63

"I don't guess we had," Longarm agreed. "You'd best go back to your bedroll now, and we'll all catch forty winks. Because soon as the first crack of daylight shows, we'll have to be on our way."

# Chapter 6

"You ladies can't be one bit gladder'n I am to see them fellows working down there," Longarm told his companions as he reined in the buggy and gestured toward the busy scene below.

"I can't speak for Retta," Dawn said. "But I'm both glad and sorry."

"I guess you can say I feel like Dawn does, Longarm," Retta said with a frown. "Glad and sorry at the same time. We've gotten to the place we were looking for, but it means we'll have to tell you good-bye."

"Oh, I ain't glad about that," Longarm said quickly. "But it means we'll be setting down on something softer'n this hard-seated buggy and moving on to where we know we're headed, instead of wondering where we are."

They fell silent, looking at the activity in the wide strip of cleared ground below them. Wagons were moving slowly along the smoothed earthen floor of the roadbed. They were loaded with wooden ties that shone yellow in the bright morning sunlight. As they advanced, men in the wagon beds were rolling ties off the tops of the load, while laborers on the ground lifted the squared lengths of wood and positioned them across the graded strip. A short distance behind the wagons other workers moved equally slowly, one on each side of the roadbed, dragging sacks of metal tie-plates behind them, stopping to place the plates at the ends of each cross-tie.

Longarm went on. "Seeing them fellows doing the kinda jobs they are means we've got to where we was heading, and we'll be striking out in different directions now."

"We still don't know whether we've missed the west-bound train, or whether we'll have to wait a day or so," Dawn reminded him. "But I know we're close to the place where our little trip together stops, and I feel just as sorry to see it end as you do, Longarm. There's nothing I'd like better than to turn around and go back to where we were last night."

"I'd like that too," Retta said quickly.

"Oh, sure," Longarm said. "I wouldn't argue about it myself. But it ain't possible, and we know we got to say good-bye. I wish we didn't have to myself, but I can't think of a way to put it off any longer." When neither of the women spoke, he went on. "I guess the polite thing for me to do is give you ladies first say-so."

With a moue of distaste that she forced into a smile, Retta said, "Good-bye, Longarm."

"And good luck," Dawn added.

"Same to you," Longarm said. "Now, I ain't got nothing to lug along but my rifle and bedroll and saddlebags. They ain't all that heavy to carry, and my suitcase was checked through from Denver. It oughtta be waiting for me in Prescott. You've got them big heavy valises, so you ladies keep the buggy and roll on to wherever the mainline trains make their turnaround to head back west."

Before either of the two women could say anything more, Longarm walked to the rear of the buggy, picked up his rifle and gear from the luggage box, and headed toward the roadbed. He turned and started following it, walking beside the cleared swatch of the right-of-way. He did not look back until he reached a long curve in the freshly cut swathe, where a second cleared strip joined the one he'd been following.

This strip curved sharply to the south, and Longarm did not need to consult his map to know that it must be the right-of-way for the tracks being laid north from Prescott. Before he started into the curving section he turned back to glance over his shoulder, and saw that the buggy had disappeared.

Longarm had been walking for what seemed to him to be a very long time. Now he'd reached a point where the gentle downward curve ended and in the long straight stretch ahead he saw in the distance a huddle of small buildings. From some point beyond them the ringing of heavy sledgehammers driving spikes broke the warming early midday air.

When he reached the buildings and saw that none of them bore signs or any other informative hints as to their use or contents, Longarm went into the one nearest to him. It was hugely cavernous, and to Longarm, who'd just come in from the bright sunlight, its interior seemed darker than it really was.

It also appeared to be empty, but as Longarm scanned his surroundings more closely, he saw the yellow rays of a kerosene lamp at its far end. Its gleam was barely visible as he headed in its direction. As he drew closer he saw that the lamp was standing on a desk. A man was sitting beside it, scrabbling through the sheets of paper that littered the desktop.

"If it's a job you're looking for, you'll have to talk to the rail-crew foreman," the man said as he glanced up and saw Longarm approaching. "He's somewhere south of here along the right-of-way."

"Thanks, but I already got a job," Longarm replied. "And I'm working at it right now. My name's Long, Custis Long. Deputy United States marshal outta the Denver office."

"In case you're chasing after a wanted man that might be in one of our track crews, I'll have to give you the same answer. The man you need to talk to is Ed Johnson. Just head south along the roadbed and chances are you'll find him in one of our work gangs."

Longarm shook his head and said patiently, "Even if running down wanted men's in my regular line of work, I ain't trying to chase down nobody right this minute."

"What're you after, then?"

"Yesterday there was a bunch of passengers that left the end of the old line that runs east," Longarm explained. "They were on horseback, heading for the railhead of this new line you folks are working on from Prescott. I'm out to catch up with 'em, and I need to know how much further I might have to go."

"I'm afraid you're going to have quite a walk," the clerk told him. "Those passengers you mentioned rode through here, all right, but Prescott's something like thirty miles from where we are right now, and we're behind schedule in our track-laying, so the work trains

68

can't run this far. Come to think of it, how the devil did you get here anyhow?"

"First in a buggy, then on shank's mare," Longarm answered. "From the end of where the old main line west to California used to be."

"Yes, of course," the man replied. He shook his head as he continued. "The big brass in Chicago sure made a mistake ripping out that stretch of rail before we finished this new line. Whoever did their time-figures didn't know how long it takes to put down rail over country like this is."

"Well, now, your railroad's troubles ain't neither here nor there," Longarm went on. "All I know is that I got to move on to Prescott."

"It's not too bad a hike along the roadbed to get to the railhead. Then you can ride the rest of the way to Prescott in the accommodation train that runs between 'em every day. And if you checked any luggage through, it'll likely be waiting for you in Prescott."

"And how in tunket is a man supposed get to that railhead you're talking about? I've done enough walking to last me a while, but I ain't seen no saddle horses anyplace around here. If I had've, I'd be riding, because all I got to do to requisition one is show my badge."

"It's not likely you'll have a chance to get a horse. The few we've got aren't in a corral. All of 'em are always out working," the desk man told him. There was no sympathy in the man's voice as he went on. "Railhead's not all that far, though. You ought to make it in about an hour."

Longarm had learned long ago to accept the bad with the good. He said, "Well, if that's the way it is, I reckon it's time for me to head out. And I'm real obliged to you for setting me right."

• • •

Feeling cramped and weary as well as grimy and gritty, Longarm stepped off the accommodation train at the Prescott depot. The sun was already dropping low, the sky in the west showing the pink tinge that heralded the approaching sunset. Cradling his rifle in the crook of one arm, he picked up the suitcase which he'd been mildly surprised to find waiting for him at the railhead shed.

"Old son," he muttered as he looked from one side to the other along the busy street, "what you best do is find a hotel where you can get a bath and a hot-water shave. If you show up at Sam Clifton's office looking like a tramp, it ain't going to speak too well of how Billy Vail runs things back in Denver."

Looking around to orient himself in the town, he remembered the Hassayampa Hotel, which had been his stopping-place on the two or three brief visits he'd made to Prescott on earlier cases. He started along Granada Street, looking both ways along each intersecting street, trying to locate the hotel from memory of his earlier visits. At last he saw the sign he'd been looking for, and turned toward it.

Half an hour later, as the once-hot water that filled the cramped tin bathtub began to grow too cool to please him, Longarm stood up in the tub and stretched.

"Old son," he muttered as he reached for the towel hanging on the hook beside the tub and began wiping himself dry, "there's three things you need right now. One's a drink, which you better not stop for till you've found Sam Clifton and let him know you're here in Prescott, and the next one's a bite of supper. Then you can get started trying to run down whoever it was that sent a hired gun all the way to Denver to cut you down."

Wrapping the towel around his midsection, Longarm cracked the bathroom door open and peered both ways along the corridor. It was deserted. He took the three long steps that brought him to his room, and made quick work of dressing. Refreshed but getting hungrier by the minute, he stopped at the hotel desk in the cramped lobby.

"I reckon I better make sure that I ain't forgot where the United States marshal's office is," he said. "It's been a spell since I was here the last time, and all I recall is that it used to be real close to the capital building."

"It still is," the clerk nodded. "Turn right when you leave the hotel, go two streets up, that'll be Palace. Just look for Matt's Saloon, it's on the corner. Walk on down to the east along Whiskey Row—its proper name's Montezuma Street—to Gurley, there you turn right to the Territorial Capital. The U.S. marshal's place is just beyond it."

"Many thanks," Longarm said. "The way you put it, I don't guess I could miss it."

Following the clerk's directions, Longarm walked briskly through the gathering dusk. Each time he passed one of the saloons on Whiskey Row he was tempted to step in and have a drink and a bite from the free lunch counter he was sure he'd find in any of them, but the day was almost over and he knew he needed to hurry.

Reaching the less-than-imposing Territorial Capital, a log cabin to which rooms of unpainted lumber had been added at each end, Longarm went on to the little shack fifteen or twenty feet beyond it. A man was standing in front of its closed door, his back toward Longarm, who frowned and stopped short. The man leaned forward, his head bending. Now Longarm could see that he was

71

fastening the padlock which hung in the door's hasp.

Moving noiselessly, Longarm stepped up to the man and stopped behind him. Then he wrapped his arms around the other's biceps, pinning them to his ribs. Instead of struggling to free himself by spreading his upper arms and twisting, the man dropped to his knees. Caught off balance, Longarm had a choice of releasing his embrace or falling. He chose to let go. The man drew as he dropped and landed on one knee. He swiveled, bringing up the muzzle of his revolver.

Longarm made no effort to draw, but stood smiling as the kneeling man lowered the muzzle of his Colt while a grin as broad as the one Longarm was showing creased the other man's face and he said, "That was a damn fool thing to do, Longarm! Why, hell's bells, if I hadn't recognized you about two seconds after I started drawing down to shoot, I might've killed you!"

"Oh, I was right sure you'd look before you pulled trigger, Sam," Longarm said. "And I was more'n just a mite curious to see if that Sam Clifton draw you're so proud of had slowed up any."

"Well, has it?"

"Not as I could tell," Longarm replied.

"How about yours?" Clifton asked.

"I'm still walking around, and I ain't got no more bullet holes in me than I had the last time we seen each other."

"Which was a pretty good spell back," Clifton said.

Longarm nodded. "Pretty much of a stretch. On the train while I was coming here I was trying to recall when was the last time we worked a case together, and it's been close to a couple of years."

"I'd say that us getting together again calls for a drink," Clifton suggested. "Now, I've locked up the office for the

72

day, so why don't we just mosey down to Whiskey Row and lift our elbows a time or two?"

"Sounds good to me," Longarm replied. "And while we're going through town, maybe you can show me where there's a barbershop. I ain't noticed one yet, and I'll need a shave in the morning worse'n I do now. All I had time to do after I got a room in a hotel was to take a bath and get rid of a pound or so of trail dust."

"Which hotel are you stopping at?"

"If I could say the name, I'd tell you." Longarm smiled. "What it sounded like to me is a doctor telling some fellow he's sick, that he's got something or other."

A frown that started to form on Clifton's face was suddenly transformed into a grin. He said, "I'll bet you a dollar to a dime you're trying to say Hassayampa."

"Now you called it," Longarm said.

"Hassayampa," Clifton repeated. "It's the name of an Indian tribe that used to live in these parts. Which doesn't keep it from being a good hotel. But right now I'm curious about the case that's brought you here. How come Billy Vail didn't just send me a wire to take care of it?"

"It's a sorta mixed-up case," Longarm said. "And I got caught in the mix-up. But it's a right long story, with a lot of whys and wherefores tied up with it. You know this territory better'n I do, so maybe you can sorta straighten things out."

"Then, let's save our breath till we've had a drink or two," Clifton said as they started walking down the graveled street side by side.

"Sure," Longarm agreed. "But before I forget it, Billy Vail wanted me to be sure and say hello for him, and tell you how glad he is you got your promotion."

"He's not anywhere near as glad as I am," Clifton said. "I needed that step up, because I got my eyes set on the prettiest little girl I ever run into. Now I can afford to marry her."

"Well, if that's what you want, I guess I'm glad for you, Sam. Maybe you'll introduce us before I go back to Denver."

"You can just bet I will," Clifton agreed.

They were passing the Territorial Capital now, and Longarm nodded toward the weatherbeaten building. "You get along all right with all the high muckety-mucks here, I guess?"

"More or less. Governor Tritle's a Republican, but that doesn't mean he's all bad. I give him credit for being a fair man. I get riled up at him now and then, because he's not much for moving fast. When he's up against a hard nut to crack, it takes him a while to make up his mind."

"Are you just talking in general, or have you got something in particular that's bothering you?" Longarm asked.

"Maybe a little bit of both," Clifton said. "What I've got in mind is that he's not putting a check-rein on a lot of little range wars that've started in Pleasant Valley. That's over east a ways, just this side of the Mogollon Rim."

"That's country I don't know too much about," Longarm observed. "But wherever there's cattle ranches, I guess you got to look for range wars, ranchers fighting among themselves."

Clifton nodded. "Oh, sure. And for a lot of reasons, like Indian reservation boundaries, water rights, stray steers getting branded by somebody they don't belong to—even a little dust-up in a saloon can start one bunch

74

of ranch hands shooting at another one. It looks like just about anything that happens sets off a new fight between 'em."

They'd reached Whiskey Row by now. It was lighted by splashes of lamp-glow that escaped from the tops and bottoms of the swinging doors of saloons which seemed to occupy every building on both sides of the street. There was a constant flow of pedestrians on the graveled thoroughfare, most of them either going into or coming out of one of the drinking oases.

"I don't suppose it makes much difference which one of these places we go into for a drink before we have supper," Clifton said. "I favor Matt's place myself. It gets a little better class of trade than most of the others."

"Well, you know the territory," Longarm replied. "And I don't much care where I drink, as long as I get some good Maryland rye. Lead the way, and I'll go right along."

Longarm and Sam Clifton were seated at a back-wall table in Matt's Saloon. The evening was just beginning, and most of the other small tables that stood in the center of the sawdust-covered floor were unoccupied, but men stood three-deep at the bar that stretched along the opposite wall. Clifton was listening and refilling their glasses while Longarm gave his fellow marshal a brief summary of the efforts made to kill him in Denver by the gunman he knew only as Frank Smith. He'd just finished telling Clifton about the check he'd inspected at the Denver bank when Clifton broke in.

"You mean there are names on that check you told me about?" he asked. "Real names?"

"Oh, there's names on it," Longarm said. "Redford Trent and Frank Smith. But sure as God made little green apples, they're just made-up ones."

"I won't argue with you about that," the Arizona marshal said. "Not just because I've never heard them before, but because it's the only sensible answer."

"You told me a while ago them ranchers that's fighting each other in that range war keep on bringing gunmen in. The fellow that had that check cashed was a hired gun, if ever I seen one. You got some names you can recall?"

"Ranchers? Or professional killers?" Clifton asked.

"I'm sorta curious about both of 'em," Longarm said. "But the gunhands are a good place as any to start. You care to put names on a few?"

"For openers, Curly Bill Brocius and Billy Thompson, and Johnny Ringo." Clifton frowned. "I guess there's more, some I haven't heard of, and I haven't set eyes on any of them myself."

"How about the Frank Smith?" Longarm asked.

Clifton looked at Longarm, and after a moment said, "You're really serious about finding who's trying to get you killed, aren't you?"

"Wouldn't you be?" Longarm countered. "Seems like I wouldn't need to cross no T's nor dot no I's for you to see that, Sam. Old hands like you and me, well, maybe we've cut down more'n our share of killers and outlaws. Thing is, we done it face to face, in a fair and square shoot-out. But lots of these Johnny-come-lately gunhands ain't like that. They're backshooters. And if I can help it, I don't aim to go down with a bullet in my back!"

As though Longarm's remark had been a stage cue, a shot rang out from the direction of the doorway. A bullet whistled across the narrow table between Longarm and Clifton. It hit the whiskey bottle that stood between them and thudded into the wall with a splatting thunk while the liquor from the broken bottle sent up a pungent-smelling spray that splashed on the wall and table as well as on Longarm and Clifton.

# Chapter 7

Although their movements were hampered by the small table between them, Longarm and Clifton managed to slide from their seats and take cover under the tabletop. They were still scrambling to free their arms and get their legs straightened out when a second shot sounded. This time a yell of pain came from the back of the saloon.

"Whoever that damn fool is, he's shooting wild," Longarm commented. His voice was level, almost casual, as he went on. "And if we don't get him first, he's likely to take down one of us instead of just spilling a lot of good drinking whiskey."

"I can see one thing stopping us," Clifton said. He was stretched out, his head raised as he tried to get a glimpse of the batwings, the moving figures of the saloon's scattering customers obscuring his view. "We can't get a bead on him from where we are now."

"Then let's move to someplace where we can do better," Longarm suggested. He started to get to his feet, but Clifton reached out and put a hand on his shoulder.

"You stay here," the Arizona marshal told Longarm. "I know the layout of this place. You cover me. Those little tables in the middle of the room are where I'll be heading."

"Any reason why I can't go along?"

"We've got to get that fellow at the door in a cross fire," Clifton said without taking his eyes from the batwings. "But we can't do that without one of us moving, and I figure it ought to be me. Don't worry, I'm going to keep my skin whole."

Before Longarm could object, Clifton started crawling, belly down, pulling with his elbows and pushing with his knees as he inched across the sawdust-strewn floor. He'd covered about a third of the distance when the gunman in the batwings fired again. The slug raised a spurt of sawdust as it plowed into the floor beyond the Arizona marshal.

Longarm had been primed for just such a chance as the one he was now offered. Before the echoes of the unknown shootist's revolver died away, Longarm had levered himself free of the hampering table legs. Flicking his eyes toward the door, he got a fleeting glimpse of the man standing in it with a leveled revolver, and raised his own Colt.

Longarm's shot reverberated through the saloon. The gunman in the door reeled, turned and vanished, but during the instant required for him to make his getaway Longarm had seen their attacker's shoulders jerk and knew that his lead had scored.

"I'm going after that son of a bitch, Sam!" Longarm called to Clifton. "I didn't bring him down, but he's hurt!"

"Go ahead!" Clifton replied. He was rising to his feet as he spoke. "I'll be right alongside you!"

Longarm was closer to the door than his fellow marshal. He reached it while Clifton was still battling his way through the tables and chairs strewn across the sawdust-sprinkled floor. Bursting through the batwings and holding his Colt ready, Longarm flicked his eyes as he searched the area around the saloon. The walls of the buildings on each side of him were too close to allow even a starving cat to slip between them. He scanned the street, but saw nobody running. Most of the onlookers were standing still, gazing at the saloon's batwings.

"Old son, that damn gunhand who was out to get either you or old Cliff could be any one of them people," Longarm muttered as he turned his searching glances from one side of the narrow street to the other. "But was I doing the kind of job he was trying to take care of, I'd've made certain sure that I had a bolthole picked out somewhere real close by."

Clifton came out of the saloon and stopped at Longarm's side. He spoke. "Got away, did he?"

"Clean as a new-washed baby's butt, Cliff. Look for yourself out there in the street, see if you can spot him. I already took a look, but I sure can't tell one of them fellows from another."

After a sweeping glance at the people milling in the street, the Arizona marshal shook his head as he turned back to Longarm. "The odds just aren't with us this time. But at least that fellow wasn't able to stop your clock."

"What makes you so sure it was me instead of you that he was after?" Longarm asked.

"If he'd been after me, he'd likely have waited till I came out of my office and potshotted me where there weren't so many people to see him," the Arizona marshal replied. "There've been two or three crooks that tried that trick, so before I step outside my office or my door at home, I take a pretty close look around."

"I'd say you're being sensible," Longarm observed. "But I guess you didn't get a clear look at whoever was shooting at us either."

Shaking his head, Clifton replied, "Even if I was looking right at him when I aimed, I was a lot more interested in watching how he might move than I was what he looked like."

"So was I," Longarm replied. "I couldn't give him a real once-over."

"Anyhow, from where I was sitting, I never did get a good look at the door," Clifton went on. "And I dived down just about the same way you did when he let off his first shot."

"I don't reckon you got any ideas about where he headed for when he ran?"

"Oh, I've got some ideas, but I don't know how good they are," Clifton said thoughtfully. "This part of town's where the rowdies and crooks hang out. There's a dozen places right close by where he could've holed up."

Longarm nodded. "I figured that, with all the saloons and the red lights in the windows I seen while we was coming here."

"Now, any other time," Clifton went on, "I'd say the thing for us to do is split up and poke our heads into every saloon and whorehouse up and down the street looking for him, but I'd bet that the son of a bitch had a hole all picked out to dive into before he ever pulled a trigger on us."

"And if I was a betting man, I'd lay a cartwheel to a plugged penny that it wasn't but one of us he was looking for," Longarm said thoughtfully. "That one being me. Except I can't figure out how he'd know where to look."

"Likely he spotted you pretty much by accident right after you got into town," Clifton suggested. "I don't suppose the way you figure's much different from the way I do."

Longarm shook his head. "Like the old saying goes, crooks are crooks the world around. I'd say all we can do is finish that drink we didn't get a chance to do more than taste, and then call it a day."

With only the slightest hesitation, Clifton nodded. "Likely you're right. There's not any use that I can see for wasting time searching. But I don't think he'll make another try, at least not this evening."

"I still ain't asked you all of the questions I got in mind," Longarm said as they settled down at the table they'd deserted so hastily. Around them, the stir of excitement that had followed the gunfire was already subsiding.

"Ask away," Clifton invited.

Longarm reached in his pocket for the folder which contained his badge and identification papers. He fingered out the slip of paper on which he'd jotted down the information gleaned from the bank in Denver and unfolded it.

"You got the name of Frank Smith on any of your want lists?" he asked Clifton.

"You know just like I do, there's more Smiths on any want list than you can shake a stick at," he told Longarm. "And I'd bet dollars to doughnuts that the list in your own office back in Denver has got ten times more names on it than mine. What does this Smith you're talking about look like?"

"He was deader'n a doornail when I seen him," Longarm replied. "But he still looked mean. Dark-complected, brown eyes. Just an ordinary kind of nose and mouth, but he had a long jagged scar along his left jaw. I'd say he got it in a knife fight quite a spell ago."

Clifton thought for a moment, frowning, then shook his head. "If I've ever run across him, I can't place him. And I'd have to go through a lot of wanted fliers to dig out all the crooks on them that claim to be Smiths. Was this dead one you mention from around here?"

"Well, me and Billy Vail turned out a money belt he had on, and besides one hell of a big wad of money, there was an envelope in it that had a Phoenix postmark. That envelope's where we got his name from."

"Then what makes you think somebody here in Prescott would be gunning for you? Why, Phoenix is better than sixty miles from here!"

"Why, I just asked on the off chance you might've run across him," Longarm replied. "When you've got as little to go on as I got in this case, the smart thing to do is grab at anything that pops up."

Clifton nodded. "It's the kind of chance I've taken more than a few times, Longarm."

"Then before I quit throwing questions at you, I'll toss out one or two more," Longarm went on. "You know anything about a fellow named Redford Trent?"

"Trent," Clifton repeated thoughtfully. "Redford Trent." Then he shook his head. "Nope. That one doesn't ring a bell either."

"Then try this one. Have you ever heard about an outfit anyplace in the Territory that's called Territorial Enterprises?"

"I can't say I have," the Arizona marshal replied. "Just what kind of business is it?"

"For all I know right now, it could be anything. It's just one of those names I had to go on. I was sure hoping I'd find out some of 'em here, but maybe I'll run into better luck when I get to Phoenix."

"You'll be heading out on tomorrow's train, I suppose?"

"Sure. I guess you got a deputy in Phoenix?"

Clifton nodded. "His office is the post office building and his name's Ned Blaine. He's a mite green, but he keeps trying, and I figure he'll make a good man someday."

"I'll look in on him, then," Longarm said. "Now, let's have this drink. Maybe this time we'll even get a chance to swallow it."

"I guess if folks got a hankering to live out in a desert like this, there ain't much of a way to stop 'em," Longarm commented. He was leaning back in a chair across the narrow table from Ned Blaine, the deputy marshal stationed in the Phoenix office. "But I ain't so sure I'd want to be here the rest of my life, with nothing much to look at but sand dunes and rocks."

"Everybody says it'll be different when we get plenty of water," Blaine protested.

"Seems to me like I recall somebody saying that about Hell," Longarm said, smiling to take any sting out of his remark. "But water's not what I come looking for. Did you ever run into a fellow named Redford Trent around here?"

After a moment of thoughtful frowning, Blaine shook his head. "No, I can't say I have, and to save you asking,

85

I don't remember seeing his name on our want list."

"That don't surprise me a whole lot. Before I left Denver, Billy Vail told me he wasn't going to put Trent's name on the list just yet, not till I find out more about him."

"So really all you've got now is a name?" Blaine frowned.

"That's about the size of it. Far as we could tell back there, we don't have a single solitary thing to charge that Trent fellow with. All we got for evidence is that a bank in Denver cashed a check he wrote and a day or so later a hired killer come gunning for me."

"But you got him first?"

"Me and Billy Vail finished the killer off in a shootout," Longarm answered. "We found a wad of cash and a letter in a half-torn-up envelope in his money belt. The letter said something about the money being a payoff for shooting me."

"And you got this Trent fellow's name off the envelope?"

"It wasn't all that easy. You see, his name wasn't on the envelope or on the little scribbled note we found in it. But that note mentioned a check, so I turned up the bank in Denver where it'd been cashed and that's where Trent's name come from."

"Then you really can't prove anything, can you?" Blaine said. "And if this Trent fellow's as cagey as I take him to be from what you've said, he'll be careful not to leave a trail that might lead to him."

"Sure, I've thought about that," Longarm agreed. "But Billy Vail figured we better find out who in tunket Trent really is and why he wants me dead, because that's got to be a sign there's some kind of crookedness back along the way. Billy and me both figure it's more'n likely something this Trent fellow's trying to work here."

"Well, Arizona Territory's got more than its share of swindlers and crooks and gunmen," Blaine said thoughtfully. "And there's generally a gunfight or two every day somewheres close around."

"That's what your chief told me when we visited up in Prescott," Longarm told him. "But he didn't dot no I's nor cross no T's. The fact of the matter is, I didn't just come here to Phoenix because crooks generally flock to towns like this one, just beginning to grow up. I got a bit of business to tend to before I can get very far along on this case."

"Case or no case, I'm afraid you headed in the wrong direction, Longarm," Blaine replied. "Didn't Sam say anything about the trouble they're having up along the Mogollon Rim?"

"He did," Longarm answered. "But I don't rightly see that what's going on up there would have anything to do with this case I'm on."

"I suppose not," Blaine said. "But that's where the hardcases and the gunhands are flocking now."

Longarm was silent for a moment, frowning thoughtfully. At last he asked, "Which side of the rim is it you're talking about? As I recall, there's good rangeland south of the drop-off and rough country to the north of it."

"Your memory's good," Blaine said. "I suppose you've worked a case or two up in that direction?"

Longarm nodded. "One or two, but not lately. And they were mostly to the north, in that rough broken-up country outlaws likes to hole up in. But I'd imagine you know the lay of the land up thataway better'n I do."

"It's still outlaw country," Blaine told him. "Close enough to the ranches on those good grazing grounds below the rim for a bunch of rustlers to drive a herd of stolen cattle over the rim and on up to Indian country where they can sell 'em."

Longarm sat silently for a moment, his forehead wrinkling and his eyes half-closed. At last he said, "You know, while we were talking it just popped into my mind that I might've moved sorta backwards when I come here."

Blaine thought for a minute. Then he spoke. "Meaning you think the man you're after might get his money somewhere else and just do his banking here?"

"That's about the size of it," Longarm answered. "But I'll know whether I'm right or not after I get through talking to the folks at the bank tomorrow."

"I'm sorry that you've been kept waiting, sir," the chubby man behind the oversized and over-polished desk in a corner of the Security Bank lobby said as Longarm settled into the chair across from him. "But what can I do to help you? A new account perhaps?"

"Not this trip," Longarm replied. While he was taking out his wallet he flicked his eyes over the brass sign on the desk. It read, "Jonathan Parker, President." Opening the wallet, he flipped it open to show his badge. "If you'll take a look that this badge, Mr. Parker, you'll see I'm a deputy United States marshal, and you can read my name off of my badge."

"Yes, of course, Marshal Long," Parker said. "I assume you're here on business, but I can't imagine what it might be. I don't recall any reason for you to visit us unless you're interested in opening an account."

"A man in the kind of job I hold don't run to bank accounts," Longarm said. "What I'm after is finding out a thing or two about one of your customers."

"Surely a man holding your position would understand that all banking transaction are private matters," Parker told him. "Transactions between our patrons and our bank are completely confidential."

"Now, it's real odd that the man at the bank in Denver who gave me two names that were on a check from your bank here didn't tell me that," Longarm said.

Parker's frown deepened. He sat silent for a moment, gazing fixedly at Longarm, who sat without changing his expression as he waited for the banker's reply. When Parker spoke again, his voice was not as gelatinous as it had been when he and Longarm began their conversation.

"Different banks and different regions may have different rules," he said. Parker's voice was harder now, without the almost effusive politeness that it had held when he first greeted Longarm. He went on. "I've explained the rules by which the Security Bank bank operates, Marshal Long. I must refuse to comply with your request. Now, if you have no more questions to ask me, I'll bid you good day."

"Well, you sure ain't left me room to ask you no more questions," Longarm told the banker. "But law's better'n rules any day of the week and twice on Sunday. Instead of asking questions, maybe I better tell you something that might not've occurred to you. If I leave here without you telling me more'n you have, which ain't much, I'll be taking you with me."

"Now, just a moment!" Parker protested. "You can't—"

"I sure as hell can!" Longarm snapped. "I'll arrest you and haul you to the closest Federal judge that's around. I'll just swear out a hold warrant and have him lock you up in a cell till you come across with the names you say you ain't of a mind to give me."

"But you can't do that!" the banker exclaimed.

"Just give me a reason why not!" Longarm snapped. He reached for the handcuffs looped around the back of his gunbelt and tossed them on the banker's desk. As their metallic clanking ended he went on, his voice hard. "Either you tell me, or you go to jail!"

For a moment Parker stared at the gleaming steel of Longarm's handcuffs. Then he said, "This is just some kind of bluff you're trying to pull, Marshal Long! It doesn't frighten me a bit!"

"Oh, I wouldn't want to scare you," Longarm told him.

His voice was deceptively mild, but before he'd finished speaking he moved with lightning speed, picking up the handcuffs and snapping one of the pair around the banker's wrist. Parker tried to pull his arm free, but Longarm's grip on the other steel circlet was firmer than Parker's.

"Look here, you can't do this, Federal marshal or not!" Parker protested.

"Why, I'd say I already done it," Longarm replied, his voice still mild.

He gave the handcuff he held a none-too-gentle yank and the banker was forced to thrust his free hand down to the desktop to keep from falling.

"Now, you can talk or you can come along to jail," Longarm told him. "It's up to you."

# Chapter 8

"I want my lawyer!" Parker exclaimed. He spoke loudly, almost shouting.

In the lobby the low hum of conversations between the bank employees and customers stopped as they turned to stare, looking for the source of the high-pitched voice. One of the tellers started out of his cage, but Parker waved him back with his free hand. Turning to Longarm again, he spoke in a more subdued and lowered tone, but his voice still reflected his surprise and showed the strain he was feeling.

"If you'll take your handcuff off my wrist, I'm prepared to discuss the draft which you mentioned a moment ago."

"You sure you feel like talking?" Longarm asked.

"Quite sure. Just get this damned thing off me."

Wordlessly, Longarm unlocked the cuff and freed the imprisoned wrist. He did not put the handcuffs away, but sat holding them in his hand as he settled into the chair which Parker had indicated with a gesture. For a few moments, the banker stared at Longarm without speaking.

"Exactly what is it you want to know?" he asked at last.

"Likely I'll want to know a lot more'n you can tell me," Longarm replied. "But that ain't neither here nor there. Right now, I'll settle for you giving me the real name of whoever it was sent a right sizeable draft on your Security Bank here to a hired killer in Denver."

"I suppose that in your position you aren't forced to tell me why you're asking." Parker's voice had lost its edge as well as its barely concealed hostility. When Longarm's expression did not change, he went on. "But I think you should explain your reason a bit more thoroughly."

Longarm said, "That check was blood money. Whoever made it out gave it to a backshooting son of a bitch that tried to cut me down. Right now, I don't aim to dot no I's nor cross no T's, but if you're so all-fired concerned about why I'm interested, I guess you'll see why."

"Now, I knew absolutely nothing about what you call blood money!" Parker protested. "We don't ask our customers questions about the money we look after for them, or the checks they write against an account. Not unless they're asking us for a loan from the bank."

"I ain't one of your customers. And I ain't accused you of a thing. What's more, I don't aim to, at least not yet," Longarm said. He held a tight rein on his temper as he went on. "Now, all I want to know is who sent the check. If you can't tell me that, I know you can give me the name of whoever's bank account the money come out of. Then I'll have one more question, and I'll put it to you right now along with everything else I'm asking. I want you to tell me where I can find the fellow that signed the check for it. After you've give me all the answers, I'll leave you free as a breeze to go on about your business."

His voice thoughtful, the banker replied, "Now that you've explained the circumstances, I'm sure I'd be justified in giving you the information you're after."

"I sorta figured you might see it the same way I do," Longarm said. "And just to save time, I wrote down what I know already." He took out his wallet and extracted a slip of paper, which he passed to Parker.

After glancing around the lobby and seeing that the tellers were conducting business as usual, the banker said, "I'll have to look at our files, if you'll excuse me just a moment."

Studying the slip of paper Longarm had given him, Parker went to the back of the bank and disappeared behind a partition. He reappeared in a surprisingly short time, and came directly to the desk where Longarm was waiting.

"That check you're interested in was cashed by the—"

Longarm broke in to say, "Begging your pardon, Mr. Parker, I already found out what you're getting ready to tell me. That check you got there was handed in at the Colorado National Bank in Denver. The fellow that cashed it was a hired gunhand traveling under the name of Frank Smith. What I want to know now is whether the name signed to this check is the real name of the man that made it out. And whether it is or it ain't, I want to know where I can find him."

"Redford Trent?" the banker asked. He shook his head. "As far as I know, that is his real name. But I'm afraid I can't be of much help to you in finding him, Marshal Long."

"Maybe you can tell me what he looks like," Longarm suggested. "That'd be a real help."

Shaking his head, Parker answered, "To the best of my knowledge, I've never seen Mr. Trent. He does all his banking with us by mail from up in Holbrook."

"That being the case, you've got an address of some kind for him, I reckon?"

"A post office box number, for what it might be worth to you, Marshal."

"I might as well have it," Longarm said. "Maybe the postmaster up at Holbrook knows what this Trent fellow looks like."

"Of course he would," Parker replied. "And that's one thing I almost overlooked. Trent's post office box in Holbrook is number seventeen."

"I guess I've just about wound up my job here then," Longarm told the banker as he stood up. "I do thank you for your help, Mr. Parker. I hope you ain't too put out because I had to be a mite rough right at the start, but you got to admit you didn't leave me much choice."

"Now that I've learned that your case is quite probably a matter of attempted murder and grand larceny, I can understand why," the banker assured him. "And if we can be of help to you, you'll find we're very happy to have you call on us."

Longarm acknowledged the invitation with a nod and returned to the street. During the short time required for him to reach the door, he'd made up his mind. A short distance ahead, he saw a sign, "LIVERY STABLE." He headed for the sign and the ramshackle building it was on. A look at Longarm's badge and the gold double eagle he offered as a deposit against a horse and saddle gear proved very persuasive to the stable hand. Before a half hour had passed Longarm was mounted and on the trail north to Holbrook.

Longarm reined in his horse to let the tiring animal rest. This was the third day he'd been in a strange saddle, jolted after having ridden from early that morning until now, when the rays of the low declining sun were about to give way to darkness. When it felt the reins tighten, the horse tossed its head as it halted and snorted vigorously, its nostrils dilating as it inhaled.

"If you were sniffing because you smell fresh water, I'd sure like to know it," Longarm told the animal. "Good water that ain't alkalied. But seeing as you ain't even trying to move, I doubt you're smelling water, so I'll just have to do the best I can for you myself."

Dismounting, Longarm took the canteen that was lashed by saddlestrings to the pommel of his saddle. It weighed less than he'd anticipated. He took two small swallows, sloshing the water in his mouth for a moment and relishing the wetness in spite of its warmth and alkaline taste.

Taking off his hat, Longarm held it by the tip of its crown while he poured in most of the water remaining in his canteen. He capped the canteen carefully and let it drop to the ground, then stepped up to the horse's head. Pushing the hat over the animal's nose, he held it in place until the few faint slurping noises ended and the horse lifted its head.

Shaking the hat to remove the droplets of water that remained in it, he replaced it on his head and secured the canteen to its improvised cradle of saddlestrings. He swung into the well-worn saddle and toed the horse into a steady walk. It was the same slow pace he'd kept the animal to through the long hot days of traveling over baked soil that was almost as hard as the small boulders that studded it here and there.

Though the horse's pace was slow, it ate up distance. Longarm had been moving for the better part of a half hour, and during that time the sun had dropped until now the bottom of the luminous disk was almost touching the jagged horizon-line. Ahead the ground was rising again, another gentle upward slant. When he topped the crest, Longarm blinked his eyes to be sure of what he was seeing.

A short distance away, directly in front of him, the stalks of green shoots covered the ground. Here and there the growth was scanty, but for the most part they were dense, hiding the yellowish brown earth. Still further ahead Longarm saw a few steers scattered widely over the ground, their heads lowered as they grazed. In the far distance he could see a broken skyline, and near the point where it met the horizon it was tinged with the deeper blue of approaching night.

What drew his attention more than the sky or sun or ground was the triangle of a roof, just visible in the fading light above the narrowing horizon-line. Longarm slapped the reins on the horse's withers to speed it to a faster walk and headed for the dwelling.

Reaching his objective was not as easy or as quick as Longarm had thought it would be. There were wide cracks in the scantily covered soil to circle around, and the light was fading steadily, more rapidly than it had been only a few moments earlier. The last rays of the disappearing sun were changing from gold to a dark orange hue and dusk was turning into darkness when Longarm could at last see the bulk of the dwelling ahead.

No light showed inside the house. Longarm reined his horse to an even slower gait, and brought it to a halt when he got within hailing distance of the small building. By this time the sky was an even deeper blue overhead, and beyond the house the horizon line had faded to a narrow jagged strip of pale purple. Longarm studied the little structure, but all that he could make out now was the outline of its roof and the oblong black patch of a door.

"Hello in the house!" Longarm called. "Anybody home?"

"Who's asking?" a woman's voice answered after a moment of silence.

"My name's Long, ma'am," he answered. He stopped at that point, made a quick decision, and went on. "I ain't here to make no trouble. I just need to make sure of whereabouts I'm at and which way I oughtta be heading to get to Holbrook."

"Well, you still got a ways to travel," she replied. "Suppose you tell me what your business is."

Evading a direct reply until he could gather a bit more information about the cabin's occupant, he answered within truthful limits by saying, "Like I said, I'm heading for Holbrook. There's some men there I need to find."

"That don't tell me much about you," the woman called after a moment of waiting. "You come here figuring to hire out?"

"Oh, I got a job," he told her. "But if you're looking to hire a hand, and you're ready to take on the first one that shows up, I figure you're on the right side of the law. So am I, if that's what's bothering you."

Reluctance showing in the tone of her voice, she said, "Well, I don't guess it'll hurt none if you come up by the

97

door here, where I can see who I'm talking to. But don't you try to get too near or come inside, just close enough so's I can get a better look at you. You stop before you get right up at the house. And I got a rifle on you, so don't try no tricks!"

As brief as it had been, Longarm's exchange with the unseen woman in the cabin had eased his mind about being in danger of stepping unawares into an outlaw hideout. He toed his horse ahead, and pulled up a scant two yards from the door. The light had faded as night continued to take the land, and the interior of the cabin was in darkness. Longarm made no effort to dismount or to doff his hat. He spread his arms to show his empty hands.

"I ain't taken out my badge because I didn't want to let you think I was reaching to draw my pistol," he said. "But I'm a deputy United States marshal, heading for Holbrook on a case. If you feel like you need to see my badge, I'll be glad to show it to you."

Now the woman who'd remained invisible inside stepped into the doorway. She had a rifle in her left hand, holding it just above the breech. Her dress was a spotted dark gingham, its long skirt almost touching the bottom sill of the cabin's door. She was both tall and thin, her gray hair backswept and done up in a small bun. Her face was narrow, her chin firm, her lips a thin line that was almost invisible. Her nose was straight, her eyebrows sparse, her dark eyes fixed steadily on Longarm.

"You say you're a Federal marshal," she said. "Maybe you'd like to tell me your name and show me your badge before you get out of your saddle."

"I'm Custis Long, ma'am," he replied, fumbling his wallet out of his pocket as he spoke and flipping it open before holding it up for her inspection. "You ain't seen me around here before because I work out of the Denver office, but I guess there's still light enough for you to see my badge. I'm heading for Holbrook on a case I'm working."

"I can see your badge plain enough to satisfy me," the woman replied. "My name's Effie Sparks. And now that I'm sure who you are, you can dismount. There's a big spike nailed up in the wall between the door and the corner window. Hitch your horse to it and step inside while I light the lamp."

By the time Longarm had dismounted and looped his horse's reins around the oversized nail that had been driven into the cabin wall, the yellow glow of lamplight was streaming through the door. He stepped inside and glanced around.

A small iron cookstove stood in a back corner of the small room, the stovepipe riding only head-high to a bend that led through the cabin wall. There was a coffeepot on the stove, and an ironware skillet as well. A double bed occupied one corner, a cot was in the corner behind the door, and in the opposite corner there was a small wardrobe chest. A round table with two straight chairs pulled up to it was between the door and the stove. Two more chairs had been pushed against the wall. The only window in the room was the small one opposite the stove, in the front wall.

Two or three quick eye-flicks had been enough to allow Longarm to take stock of the small room and its sparse furnishings. He had not moved any further into the cabin than his first step through the door had taken him. Effie Sparks nodded toward the table.

"Set down if you ain't too saddle-sprung," she said. "But till his dying day my husband never would settle in a chair for a good while after he'd come in from a day on his horse."

"Well, there's times when I don't like to set in a chair right after I've left my saddle," Longarm said. "But you go on and set down and be comfortable. I'll take a chair in a minute or two, soon as the kinks get outta my legs."

"You've been riding a long time, I reckon?" she asked.

"All the way up here from Phoenix."

"That is a far piece. And I don't aim to pry into something that's not rightly my concern, but are you looking for somebody in particular, or just on your way home?"

"Oh, I'm on a case, all right." Longarm was making a decision as he spoke. "I reckon you know pretty much all there is to know about this part of the Territory?"

"Well, now, that depends," she said. "I know there's a lot of deviltry going on that ought not to be. And wouldn't be except for Apaches roaming off their reservation and land-grabbers and rustlers that're as bad as the redskins are. And even if it ain't nice of me to say so, crooked lawmen." Then she added quickly, "Present company always excepted, Marshal Long."

Longarm acknowledged her modification with a nod, then he said, "I don't suppose you'd mind getting down to cases and maybe even mentioning a name or two."

For a moment Effie Sparks sat silent, then she said, "You're looking for somebody in particular, you say?"

"Well, I got a little business to take up with a fellow by the name of Frank Smith," Longarm told her. "Except that I ain't all too sure that's the name he goes by here. And I don't know what he does nor much else about him."

"There's a whole passel of Smiths around here. There's one family of 'em that ranches up by the Mogollon Rim, and there's two more families of 'em in Holbrook," she said thoughtfully. "And I don't know how many more that might not've been Smiths all their lives. But right this minute, I don't recall there being a Frank Smith."

Longarm nodded. "Like I was saying a minute ago, I ain't sure the one I'm looking for is called Frank Smith in these parts, but it's about the only lead I got to tie to."

"This one you're looking for," Effie frowned. "Can you tell me why—"

She broke off suddenly as a thudding of distant hoofbeats sounded. Before she could speak again the unmistakable crack of a rifle shot sounded above the hoofbeats. Then a shrill yell rose above the drumming of hooves and another shot rang out.

Longarm was on his feet only an instant before Effie rose. He took two long strides and reached the open door before she did. He stepped outside, and the thud of horses' hooves was louder. Longarm turned in the direction of the sounds and saw the swirling of a low-lying dust cloud. The beginning darkness had deepened during the short time he'd been talking with Effie Sparks in her cabin, but before he could turn to question her she spoke.

"That's bound to be Charley!" she exclaimed. "And nobody but Apaches yells like that!"

Longarm did not waste time in replying. He was already moving toward his horse. At its side he yanked his Winchester from its saddle scabbard. As he stepped back to the door, he could see a lone rider silhouetted against the rising cloud of dust. Behind the horseman the half-visible forms of other riders could be seen, but the steadily darkening sky and the dust cloud raised by the drumming hoofbeats of the leaders made them almost invisible. The three leading riders were only a short distance behind the man galloping ahead of his pursuers. Longarm brought up his rifle, and was shouldering it when Effie reached his side.

"Don't shoot Charley!" she exclaimed. "He's my son, the only family I've got!"

Longarm replied calmly, "Don't worry, ma'am. It ain't him I'll be aiming at, and I'm a fair-to-middling shot."

Leveling the Winchester, Longarm took quick aim at the leader of the three riders outlined against the swirling dust. He triggered off his shot. The one he'd chosen for his target jerked backward in his saddle, then lurched to the ground in a sidewise fall.

Even before the man hit the ground Longarm had levered a second round into the Winchester's chamber. He aimed almost casually this time, sure now of his range. He squeezed the trigger. The silhouetted form of one of the remaining pair of leading horsemen jerked, but the man did not fall.

By this time the third leading rider was reining his mount around. Shrill yells were rising from the dust-obscured horsemen who made up the remainder of the group. The surviving lead rider reined around. As though his move was a signal for the others, they also turned. During the few moments required for their maneuvering to retreat the dust cloud had begun settling. The horseman who'd been the object of their chase had not slackened his pace. He was continuing to gallop toward the cabin.

Longarm lowered his rifle and turned to Effie. "Them redskins ain't going to stop till they get back to where they started out from," he told her. "And it don't look like your boy's hurt none. When he gets here, I reckon we'll find out how all this fracas got started."

# Chapter 9

"I don't reckon I can thank you enough for saving my boy," Effie Sparks said. "If it wasn't for you, I'd be having to dig his grave, like I did his daddy's."

"You been living here quite some spell then?"

"Since before the big buffalo herds got shot out," she replied. "That was a good while ago. Why, the Hashknife Ranch was just getting started up good when we settled this place and my husband built our cabin. There wasn't anything a body could see then from here to there but a buffalo herd now and again. Mostly you just was looking at grass and cholla cactus and a few coyotes and cougars."

"And I guess some redskins like them we just drove off?" Longarm asked.

"Oh, we saw redskins," Effie replied. "Wilder than they are now, and just as mean and ornery when they take a notion to be. But there was a lot more then. And I'll say this. It wasn't until the government started shutting them in on reservations that they got peskier than ever."

"I don't guess there was many towns around then?"

"Not any that you'd call real towns, with streets and all. Just a few little crossroads stores and a few shanties they call houses. The closest big one is Holbrook. It's new, but it's got to be a real town right fast, with streets and stores and all like that. There's two saloons and a few stores that're right nice. When we settled here it wasn't but one store and one saloon where the hands from the Hashknife did their drinking and what little trading there was to do then. It's grown a mite since those days."

"I guess they'd have a constable or somebody to stand up for the law?"

"Why, it's a county seat, and there's a sheriff and all there." Effie smiled. "The closest thing to law we've got here is way to the south of Holbrook, at Fort Apache, where there's soldiers to keep the reservation redskins behaving right."

Effie's son reached them and dismounted, and she broke off. She said, "This man's a U.S. marshal, Charley. His name's Mr. Long. It's lucky he's a good shot, or that bunch of Apaches chasing you might've got you and me both."

Longarm had been studying the new arrival. Charley Sparks was a tall rawboned young man, his face almost as bronzed as those of the Indians who'd been chasing him. His once-blue shirt was sweat-stained and faded, as were the Levi's tucked into the tops of his battered boots. Even before Effie had stopped speaking he stepped up to Longarm, his hand extended.

"I reckon I owe you, Marshal Long," he said as they shook hands. "It was sorta chancy for a while with them redskins getting closer and closer to me. A time or two I wasn't real sure I'd make it."

"I don't look for no credit just because I lent your mother a hand getting rid of them," Longarm told him. "Anybody'd have done the same thing."

"I've run across lots of redskins," young Sparks went on. "But they never jumped me as fast as this bunch did. They come pouring out of a little canyon before I knew what was going on. You sure saved my scalp."

"It wasn't nothing but luck," Longarm protested. "I just happened to be passing by, and your mother asked me in. Otherwise, I'd likely have been on my way to Holbrook. Why'd them Indians take out after you anyhow?"

"Not for anything I did to them. I was looking for a steer that'd strayed, or I figured it had. But the way those Apaches acted, I've got a hunch they'd slaughtered it and made a meal or two off of it. It's the only reason I can think of that would've started them chasing after me. I just heard a yell and looked up, and there they were."

"Well, you're home safe, Charley, and that's all I care about," Effie said. "Now, I was just about ready to ask Marshal Long if he'd care to have supper with us and stay the night."

"Now, I wouldn't want to impose on you," Longarm said quickly.

"You won't be," she assured him. "It won't be a fancy supper. All I've got ready is a nice three-day stew that I was going to warm up for me and Charley, but there's plenty for one more. It's getting on for late, and you'd have to travel half the way to Holbrook in the dark. The trail's not all that good. You'd be saving time by staying and riding on in the morning"

"Well, all that makes good sense," Longarm told her. "And if you're sure about me not being any trouble, I'll be right proud to take your kind invitation."

"And we'll be glad to have you," she replied. "So you and Charley just settle down to visit a while, and keep from getting underfoot while I'm fixing supper and setting the table."

As Longarm and Charley sat down on the doorstep, Longarm observed, "Your mother, she's a real spunky lady."

"Oh, she's that, all right," the young man agreed. "We wouldn't be here if she wasn't." He pointed to a spot some distance away from the house. "That green patch over there, where the brush has been cleared away, that's my daddy's grave."

"Is it now," Longarm said. "Died sorta young, did he?"

"He was shot and killed in a fracas between the two big ranch outfits that was in these parts then, the Blevinses and the Tewksberrys."

"I've run into some range wars myself," Longarm said as Charley paused. "And they can get real mean. Whose side was your daddy on?"

"Neither one. He was set on proving out this little spread that he'd already claimed on, and the Tewksberrys and Blevinses were both trying to get him to sell out to them. But they're both gone now. The Hashknife folks from up above the Mogollon Rim came along and bought out both of them."

"Well, how'd your daddy get killed, if he was right here on his own land where neither one of the other outfits didn't have any business being?"

"There was a bunch of hands from Blevins's spread and a bunch from the Tewksberry outfit that met up here on our place one day just by happenstance. They started out just fussing and cussing. Then one bunch or the other—nobody ever did figure out which that I know of—anyhow, they got madder and madder and started shooting at each other. Daddy got caught in a cross fire, and there he was laying dead, right where he's buried now."

"I've seen fights like that bust out before I got on the job I hold down now, and afterwards too," Longarm said when Charley sat silent for a moment. "Too bad your daddy was in between 'em."

"Even worse was that him getting shot didn't stop them two outfits from fighting," Charley said. "Ma waited a little bit and then she got mad. She picked up a shovel— that was all she had, Daddy's rifle was laying out by him where he'd dropped. But Ma didn't waste a minute. She walked right between the Blevinses and Tewksberrys and started digging Daddy's grave."

"And all the time those two bunches were still shooting?"

Charley shook his head. "They stopped when she started to walk between 'em. She dug a grave for Pa and rolled him in it and covered him up and said a prayer for him."

"And none of the hands from either bunch lifted a finger to help her?"

"Not a man. They sat in their saddles till she got back in the house, then they started shooting again. Finally the Tewksberry outfit began to run, and the Blevinses took out after them. But neither one of them ever came here to try and buy Pa's land rights again."

"So you and your mother've been here ever since, I see."

"That's about the size of it," Charley said. "We've had good days and tough ones, but it's home."

"There's times . . ." Longarm began, but fell silent when Effie called from the house.

"Come and get it, such as it is!"

Longarm and Charley moved into the house. Effie had spread the table with a red-checked cloth. A large china bowl stood in its center, plates and utensils on three sides.

"It ain't much," Effie said. "But it's what we got. So set down and pull up your chairs and eat hearty."

Now that the sun had gotten high enough in the eastern sky for Longarm's hat brim to keep its rays out of his eyes, he felt better. He was sure that before the end of the day he'd reach Holbrook, in spite of his uncertainty about the trail. After he'd left the green pastures of the Sparks place, there had been places where the trail had petered out when it crossed an especially hard-baked stretch of the featureless desert.

Although both Effie and her son had assured him that the trail leading to Holbrook was easy to follow in the daytime, even with his experience on many stretches of barren Western prairies and badlands, Longarm had not found it all that easy to keep on the nearly invisible trace. He'd lost sight of the trail more than once, but at such times had managed to stay with the faint trace by zigzagging and scanning the barren earth, looking for even the slightest marks of hoofprints.

He was always careful to keep the rising sun in his face, and until the gleaming orb rose almost halfway to its zenith, even the vaguest sign that the hard earth had been disturbed by a horse's iron shoe was enough to give him the guidance needed to stay with the trail. Now, with the sun more than halfway across the cloudless sky, it had become more and more difficult for Longarm to make out the faint hoofprints.

As yet the air was still comfortably cool, but the slow and fleeting gusts of an occasional faint swirling breeze that brushed across his cheeks told him that soon the air would be even hotter than the snakelike thread of smoke which came from the tip of the long slim cigar he'd just lighted.

In front of him a few thin feeble heat-ripples were already beginning to rise from the yellow sand that extended on all sides as far as he could see. No stranger to desert country, Longarm knew that the few scattered blobs of green which broke the monotony of the expanse of parched yellow sand were spiny cactus plants. Years ago during his first trip across the great American desert he'd learned very quickly to avoid them.

"There's one thing certain sure," Longarm said, in the habit that he'd acquired of talking aloud, addressing only himself, during many such lonely rides. "This ain't the kind of a day that makes a man want to do anything he don't have to, hot as that sun is beating down on him.

"Now, even if it's taking you longer'n you figured to get to Holbrook, old son, there's got to be water someplace up ahead, because this nag's going to need a drink just as bad as you will. But it stands to reason there's a spring or a well or even a little creek along this trail. That'd be real nice, getting outta these duds and splashing around for a spell instead of having to wash down in your own sweat. Of course, you ain't seen no sign of one yet, but it's bound to be up ahead, or this trail never would've been made."

Buoyed up by his own assurances, Longarm reached for the canteen that hung by its webbed canvas strap from his saddlehorn. He hefted it, and a frown flicked across his face. When he held the canteen close to his ear and shook it, only the faintest sloshing of liquid could be heard.

"Old son," he went on, "you ain't been minding your P's and Q's. You been swigging too much when you didn't need to since this canteen was filled up. You better just hang on to what little bit of water's left in here and keep your eyes peeled for a water hole of some sort, where you can fill it up again."

Suppressing his growing urge to drink from the canteen, Longarm let it drop to hang in its saddle-tie, and returned his attention to the almost invisible trace he was following. As the sun had risen higher in the sky it had grown increasingly more difficult for him to make out the thin faint shadows that the sun had cast earlier at the edges of the hoofprints he was following.

Until the shimmering heat-waves began rising from the constantly warming ground, Longarm had scanned the land ahead occasionally. Now, with the heat of the day increasing, even the high branching arms of the saguaro cactus, arms as big around as small barrels or kegs, rising ten to fifteen feet above the ground, were as hard to see clearly as were as those of the thin-stemmed cholla cactus which shared the otherwise barren desert landscape.

In his total concentration on following the barely visible hoofprints which were his only guide leading to his destination, watching the ground, Longarm had paid little attention to his surroundings. For the last half-mile or so, during the occasional instants when he'd raised his eyes from the trail, he'd noted the unusually large stand of high-growing thick-branched saguaro ahead and off to one side of the trail which he was still managing to follow, but in the sameness of the terrain he'd given it only an occasional glance now and then.

Suddenly an explosion of sharp-edged yells rose from the cover of the saguaro's barrel-round upthrust stalks. Longarm was reaching for his Winchester long before the shouts died away. He yanked the rifle out of its saddle-scabbard, and was bringing it up before the last of the half-dozen horseback-mounted Indians cleared the cactus which had concealed them.

Longarm wasted no precious seconds in shouldering and sighting the rifle. Dropping the reins, he leveled its barrel across the support of his left forearm. As closely huddled together as the Indians were when they broke cover to launch their attack, it would have been almost impossible for a seasoned veteran such as Longarm to have missed the shot he triggered off. The Indian in the lead lurched backward when the Winchester's slug went home. The man swayed on his mount for a few seconds before dropping to the ground.

As the riderless horse felt the Indian drop, it reared on its hind legs, then with a neighing snort it leaped ahead. Its sudden move took it to the riders that had just passed it. The panicked animal crashed into the nearest of the mounted Apaches, and the collision sent both the rider and his horse careening into a third Indian.

Though neither of the riders were knocked off their mounts, the moves of the panicked horse forced the Apaches to break their bunched-up charge. Belatedly, their attention to Longarm diverted by the spooked animal, they began to scatter. Longarm saw his chance and took it. He yanked the reins and his horse stiffened its legs, driving its hooves into the ground to stop almost instantly.

His halt gave Longarm time to pick a target for another quick shot. He leveled his Winchester at the Apache who was at the head of the group now, and in that precise instant of dead-true aim triggered it off. The Apache reared back and the reins of his mount slid from his hand. Then he toppled to the sunbaked earth and lay motionless while his horse reared and lurched into the mount of an Indian who had just swung his rifle to get Longarm in its sights.

An instant before the sharp crack of his shot sounded and the red spurt of muzzle-blast flashed, the crazed horse brushed past the Indian. There was no hard collision between the two animals, but the sudden light impact of their bodies touching was enough to throw off the redskin's aim. The slug from his rifle sang its ugly song of death as it whistled only a few inches in front of Longarm's chest to bury itself in the hard soil somewhere beyond the scene of the encounter.

Longarm paid no attention to the bullet's high-pitched whine as it sped by. He was looking for a new target, but by this time the Apaches had broken the close cluster in which they'd been when they first emerged from the stand of cactus. They were wheeling, for their mad gallop out of their cactus cover had left the survivors in awkward positions. Now they were forced to rein their mounts almost a full half circle in order to be sure of a telling shot. None of them had succeeded in their efforts yet, but Longarm was in as unhappy a position as they were, out in the open as he was.

Both Longarm and the Apaches were trying to overcome their disadvantages when the shrill brassy notes of a bugle blowing the charge sounded from somewhere on the downward slant beyond the cactus stand. The Indians

112

were between the spot beyond the rising ground where the bugle had sounded and the point where Longarm had put up his successful defense after their first surprise shot. For a moment they hesitated, and the hesitation proved to be their final undoing.

Along the crest of the rise the heads of the approaching cavalrymen were already beginning to show. Although the soldiers had topped the crest ahead and were now visible, they were still too far away from the spot where Longarm and the Indians had been trading shots for their short-barreled outdated cavalry carbines to be effective. But the speed of their approach evened the odds somewhat, and it was obvious to Longarm that the Indians also knew this.

While the redskins were milling in their hesitation, relieving him of the need to swerve his horse in an effort to evade their fire, Longarm took advantage of his opportunity. He reined in and took quick aim at the Indian who seemed to be taking command. Though the range was extreme, Longarm's bullet found a target, not in the Indian's body, but in that of his horse. The animal reared, and its whinnying of pain-induced panic sounded above the beginning crackle of shots from the cavalrymen.

For a moment the horse twirled in a dancing circle, then started toward the advancing soldiers. The Indian rider was thudding his heels on the horse's barrel, but his drumming had no effect. Then a small crackle of shots came from the soldiers and both horse and man dropped to the ground.

Longarm flicked his eyes across the rolling ground around him. The cavalry troop was now close enough for even their outdated rifles to be effective. Shots were

113

sounding almost constantly, from the diminished group of the Indians as well as from the soldiers. The redskins could not seem to find a direction in which to retreat, and with their number diminished by a third, they took the only option open that would save their lives.

One by one they threw their rifles to the ground and raised their arms, extending them widely apart to show their empty hands. Longarm brought his own rifle down as the barking of a command came from the direction of the soldiers. Suddenly the sun-warmed air of the desert was quiet.

A shouted command sounded from the direction of the small knot of cavalrymen that had not scattered during the brief firefight. The group began moving forward, approaching the spot that a moment ago had been the center of the strung-out fracas. Longarm touched the flank of his own horse with the toe of his boot, and even though its gait showed its weariness, the animal started moving toward the small group of cavalrymen.

As the distance between Longarm and the soldiers diminished, the cavalrymen who'd born the brunt of the fighting began rounding up the surviving Indians, forcing them into a compact group. The Indians did not resist, nor did any of them speak as they moved in obedience to the soldiers' shouted orders.

Longarm returned his attention to the approaching rider. As the distance between them diminished he could see the two silver bars of a captain on the shoulders of the cavalryman's sweat-soaked shirt. As the army officer got within hailing distance, Longarm raised his voice to call to him.

"You're sure a welcome sight, Captain!" he shouted. "Till you showed up, I was trying to figure out how I could get outta that fracas I was into with a whole skin!"

"Don't feel at ease too soon!" the officer called back. "Right now, I'm putting you under arrest for unlawful trespass on an area under military control!"

# Chapter 10

For a moment Longarm sat speechless in his saddle, his jaw dropping. When he'd recovered from his surprise he said, "Now just hold on a minute! If you—"

"No, you hold on!" the officer broke in. "This road's closed to everybody but official military or Indian Bureau travelers. Anybody that wants to use it has to get an official pass from the army or the Indian Bureau."

"Well, now," Longarm said. "I sure ain't a soldier and I don't work for the Indian Bureau. But I ain't a rancher or a farmer neither. Now the one place you're hitting just a little ways outta the bullseye is that I'm traveling on official government business."

Frowning, the military man asked, "Just what kind of business might that be?"

"Why, I reckon you'd say that me and you are both on the same side, Captain," Longarm replied. "My name's Long, Custis Long, deputy United States marshal outta the Denver office."

"I sure hope you can prove that," the officer replied.

"Because if you can't, you're going to be in one hell of lot of trouble!"

"All you got to do is look at my badge," Longarm told the soldier. "It'll prove just what I told you about being who I am." As he spoke he was sliding out the wallet containing his badge and duty orders. "You don't need to do more'n take a quick look and you'll see my name in that circle around the star." Flipping the wallet open, he displayed his badge.

After a glance at Longarm's badge, a single quick flick of his eyes, the soldier said, "It looks genuine enough, but how do I know you're this fellow Custis Long whose name's on here?"

"That's because I am," Longarm said curtly. "If you don't figure it's the real thing, it'd be easy enough to find out."

"How do you figure that? We're a long ways from Denver."

"Why, wherever your headquarters are at, I'd imagine you got a government telegraph line. All you need to do is send a wire to my chief and tell him you're holding Deputy Marshal Custis Long."

"Just exactly who might your chief be? What's his name?"

Without an instant of hesitation, Longarm replied, "His name's Billy Vail, and he's in charge of the Denver office, the chief marshal. You wire him asking about me, and he'll wire you back right away to tell you who I am and what's what."

"That won't be necessary," the army officer said. "Your identification's completely satisfactory, Marshal Long. My name's Eli Allison, and I guess you can see what my rank is just by looking at my bars."

"If I ain't forgot everything I knew about the army, you'd be Captain Allison then." When the officer nodded, Longarm went on. "I got a question to ask you now. I'd like to know how come you decided I wasn't lying to you after you looked at my badge."

"Why, the minute you invited me to wire Denver I knew you had to be telling the truth. No imposter in his right mind would've invited me to get the chief U.S. marshal in Denver to identify him. He'd know better than that."

"I hadn't exactly looked at it that way before, but I can see what you're driving at," Longarm said. Then, indicating the soldiers who'd scattered out to disarm the Indians, he said, "I reckon you and your men have been out looking for this bunch of redskins that jumped me?"

"My detachment's been chasing after them for two days now," the army man answered. "Ever since they sneaked away from the Indian stockade that our outfit's in charge of at the reservation headquarters back at Fort Apache."

"I guess you've got the bad ones in that stockade you're talking about?"

"They're as mean a bunch of Apaches as you'll find anywhere. They're so ornery that when they can't find anybody else to fight with they'll start a ruckus with some of the other Apaches just to keep their hand in. Why, it's been such a job keeping them from giving everybody trouble that we don't allow anybody but men from our own army on the reservation."

"Well, the only reason I'm on your reservation is because the road I got to travel over goes through it. I sure don't aim to get in your way while you're corralling them redskins that tried to stop my clock," Longarm said.

"Oh, I won't slack off on my job," Allison said quickly. "And I hope you understand that keeping these Apaches from straying off the reservation is just part of it. The other part's to keep settlers and travelers from coming onto it."

"Hold on, now," Longarm said. "I didn't see no signs telling folks to stay away. How come there weren't none, and no fences either, where the reservation lines runs?"

"Marshal Long, we don't have enough barb wire for the fences we'd need. This Apache reservation's seventy-five miles from north to south and sixty miles east to west," Allison said. "How'd you like the job of stringing barb wire all around it?"

"I'd likely say no thanks. It'd be more'n I'd care to tackle," Longarm replied.

"Then how many men do you think we've got to spare riding fence lines?"

"Not none too many, I'd imagine. I can see it's a job that'd be likely to take more men and time than you've got to spare."

"We've got two infantry platoons and one cavalry squadron. That's just a bit over a hundred men. And we've got more than half—close to two thirds—of the whole damned Apache nation to ride herd on."

"I got to admit, I wouldn't hanker one little bit to swap jobs with you," Longarm told him. "But speaking of jobs, you got one to finish here and I got one waiting for me when I get to Holbrook. I don't reckon it'd hurt nobody a bit if I angle on to the north and east across your reservation, would it?"

"It wouldn't hurt anybody but you, if you want to get to Holbrook," Allison replied. "And I don't know what kind of a map you've got, except that it's got to be dead wrong."

"Why, I don't have no map a-tall," Longarm told the officer. "Far as I know, there ain't no maps of Arizona Territory that a man can get his hands on. I tried to get one at the marshal's office in Prescott and the one in Phoenix, but I didn't have no luck. They didn't either one have a map they could spare me, and I couldn't find no place where I could buy one."

"One thing I know for sure is that you must've taken the wrong fork somewhere," Allison said. "Holbrook's not to the northeast. From where we're standing right now it's a long day's ride northwest of here. If somebody set you on this road, they sure didn't do you any favor."

Longarm's jaw dropped and he said, "The folks that told me to take the road from their ranch said there was signs all the way from their road at just about every fork. At the last fork I passed, just before dark night before last, there was a sign laying on the ground, looked like maybe somebody'd kicked it over. It had Holbrook on it, and the way it laid, it pointed along this trail I been following, so I just figured it'd be the one I oughta take."

"It sounds to me like there's been a joker at work," Allison said. "There's always a damn fool or two who thinks it's smart to shift road signs around. But if you'll walk back to my horse with me, I've got an ordnance map in my saddlebag. You can study it long enough to figure out which way you'll need to go to get to Holbrook. I imagine you're anxious to finish your trip and get started on the job you mentioned."

"Oh, I need to get there all right, but I'm not aiming to give my nag the heaves by pushing it too hard. So let's go take a look-see at your map, and I'll get myself on the right road, if there is one. The sooner I close this case of mine, the quicker I'll be getting back to Denver, where a body can move around easy and sleep nights without sweating himself to death."

"You sure had one hell of a time getting here, old son, but you finally made it," Longarm said. Following his usual habit when riding alone, he spoke aloud. "And all them lights is bound to mean you're getting close to a right fair-sized town, which'd mean certain sure that it's Holbrook. Even if it ain't, wherever it is it'll do to rest in a spell if you find out that you still got a ways to go after you get there."

For Longarm the day that was now reaching its end had been a monotonous as well as a hot one. Following the few landmarks given him by Captain Allison, he'd stopped riding only when resting the horse made it necessary. Instead of losing time by making a stop at noon, he'd dug into his saddlebags for a bite or two of dried jerky and ship's biscuits, eaten them in the saddle, and washed them down with a scant swallow of warm water from his canteen. Now, his empty stomach was sending him regular but not yet urgent inquiries about his next meal.

Keeping his eyes on the blobs of light that dotted the near distance, Longarm reined in his horse to give it the breathing spell that the animal was showing it needed after reaching the top of the long rise. From where he now sat in his saddle he could see a sprawling expanse of buildings on the surface of the low plateau in front of him. On both sides of the road a gaggle of widely spaced houses formed a somewhat ragged line along a stretch of a mile or more.

From the top of the modest rise that was now his vantage point, Longarm could see the roofs and false fronts of several stores and the upper-floor windows of the small handful of two-story buildings that rose above the straggle of houses surrounding them. There seemed to be no rhyme nor reason to their location. Some of the more substantial-looking buildings stood close to the road. Others were some distance away from it.

After a few more moments of silent study, flicking his eyes more slowly now to take in the details that his first quick glances had missed, Longarm had a reasonably good idea of the town's layout. He'd now identified its main street, and discovered the arching railroad tracks that made a sweeping curve into the central portion from the level ground north and east of the town. On both sides of the settlement the rails slanted away and vanished at the rim of the northern horizon.

"Seeing as how you ain't found out for sure yet that this is where you been heading for, you better quit lally-gagging and move along," Longarm told himself. "You been gallivanting around too long the way it is now, old son. If you don't start cutting a shuck or two, Billy Vail ain't going to be real happy when you get back to Denver. Besides that, you likely won't run into no saloons this far out from town, and a sip of good whiskey is what you need right now, after all the dry days you put in getting here."

Though Longarm's pause had been short, the rest had given his tiring horse time to breathe, and after he'd started the animal with a nudge of his boot toe, it settled into a brisk walk down the gentle slope of the trail.

Details he'd been unable to see earlier became more

clearly visible as he progressed. Except for one thing, Longarm saw little that he had not guessed he'd find during his observation from a distance. The new ingredient was the town's name on the signs that identified the stores and the kind of goods they offered. He seldom saw a merchant's name on a store, but the legend on many of them led off with "Holbrook." Aside from that one detail, the central strip of stores on the main street might have belonged to almost all the Western towns which Longarm had ever visited.

On both sides of it buildings stood close together in reasonably straight parallel rows for a quarter of a mile. Surrounding them were houses, most of them modest dwellings, but a few boasting a second story rising above the roofs.

Horses as well as an occasional wagon or buggy stood at hitch rails in front of nearly all the stores, and there was a good amount of pedestrian movement between the other types of business. Only a few of the stores were dark, and they were the ones which occupied the smaller buildings. Wide strips of light above and below busy pairs of swinging doors marked about half of the street's buildings as saloons.

"Old son, the next one of them drinking holes you come to, you better stop and get a swallow and maybe a bite of free lunch," Longarm said, his voice low, making his soliloquy barely audible.

Just ahead he saw the jumpy bursts of light that identified swinging doors. Longarm turned his horse to the rail in front of the saloon, and wrapped its reins around the rail before pushing through the batwings. Inside there were fewer than a half-dozen men bellied up to the bar that stretched across one side of the building. The lone bartender had been replacing a bottle on the shelves behind the bar. He turned and stepped down to the spot where Longarm had stopped.

"What's your pleasure, friend?" the aproned man asked.

"Straight rye, no chaser," Longarm replied. "Tom Moore, if you got some. If you ain't, I'll settle for any good Maryland rye."

Almost before Longarm had finished speaking the barkeep was turning to the back bar. He found the bottle he'd reached for with one hand while picking up a shot glass with the other, and set bottle and glass in front of Longarm.

"I always like to see a customer get what he asks for," he said. "But we get a lot of shiftless drifters here in Holbrook, so without meaning no offense I need to see some money in front of you on the bar before I pour your drink."

"No offense taken," Longarm replied, digging into his pocket. He found a gold half eagle by feel and dropped it on the counter.

Before the ringing of the gold piece had died away the barkeep was filling Longarm's glass. He shoved the glass across the bar, and was reaching for the coin when Longarm said, "You might as well take out for another one. And I'd be right pleased to stand you a shot if your boss don't object."

"Thanks," the barman replied. "And I just happen to be the boss. But I don't let my help drink while they're working, so much as I'd like to say yes to your offer, I can't set 'em a bad example and join you."

Longarm nodded understandingly and downed about half the whiskey in his glass. When he'd finished swallowing it he told the saloon-keeper, "I'll take the will for the deed. Maybe you'll let me treat you the next time I stop in."

"I'll hold you to that if I'm not working behind the bar like I am now," the saloon man said. "And I hope to see you in here again." While he spoke, his eyes were flicking over Longarm's hat and shirt, coated with trail dust and streaked with blotches where trail dust had collected in sweat-wet folds of cloth. He went on. "It sure looks to me like you've been doing some pretty good riding today. Is this the first time you've stopped in Holbrook?"

"Well, I've come through here a time or two on the train, but you don't see much of a town that way. I aim to stay a while this trip, so if you ain't too busy maybe you can tell me a thing or two I need to know while I'm having my next drink."

"You see what trade's like right now," the saloon man said, indicating the scantily patronized bar with a wave of his hand. "So go on, ask away."

"First off, it looks like I'll be here for a little spell," Longarm said. "And I'll need someplace to stay. Maybe you can tell me where a stranger in town here can find a place to put up in for the night, maybe for even longer."

"Why, sure. Your best bet's Miz Carrie Hill's boarding-house. It's clean, and she'll let you pay by the day if you want to. Her place is a big two-story building painted gray. It's just off Main Street a few squares from the sheriff's office. You can see it from the street. It'll be over to your left."

"It's funny you mentioned the sheriff," Longarm said. "I'm sorta curious about who's keeping folks straight with the law around here now." He noticed the beginning of a frown on the barman's face and added hastily, "I ain't got a thing to be spooked about where the law's concerned, but I got a lot of lawman friends that changes jobs pretty regular, and when I'm in a strange town I always ask to find out if any of 'em might be around."

For a moment the barman did not reply, then he said, "You might not believe it, but the sheriff here's named Commodore Perry Owens."

"Commodore Perry?" Longarm said. "Why, he was a sailor way back a spell. You got to be joshing me."

"It's gospel truth. Commodore Perry Owens is our sheriff's real name, and folks hereabouts have learned that he don't settle for anybody calling him just 'Commodore' or 'Perry.' Even if you're a real good friend of his, he expects you to call him Commodore Perry. Not just one of his names, but both of 'em. If he don't know you all that well, you call him Sheriff Owens, but he don't settle for nothing else."

"Well, I got a sorta nickname myself," Longarm said. "But it don't faze me for a minute when folks don't use it."

Longarm had half expected the barkeeper to question him further, but the man merely nodded. "I guess all of us are sorta quirky where names are concerned," he went on when Longarm said nothing more. "Now, my name's Benjamin Franklin Stewart, but everybody just calls me Ben, and I don't mind a bit. That's not here nor there, though, and you were asking me about our sheriff. If you've got business with him, his office is right on down the street a little ways. Just go left when you leave, it's not far."

"Got a sign in front of it, I guess?"

"Oh, yes. You can't miss seeing it."

"Well, Ben, I thank you kindly for telling me about your sheriff," Longarm said. "And I reckon that's all I need to know, so I'll be getting on about my business now, but I'll likely drop in again tomorrow."

"Be glad to see you any time," the barman replied.

Longarm mounted his horse and reined it slowly along the street, keeping his eyes on the buildings as he moved. The sheriff's office would have been a hard place for him to miss. Though the building itself was small, the sign outside it was large, and the name and title of the sheriff of Gila County far overshadowed in length and size the name of the county itself. Reining his horse off the street to the hitch rail in front of the modest building, Longarm dismounted and stepped inside.

What he saw was not what he'd expected. Longarm was accustomed to the offices used by lawmen, but this was like none he'd ever seen before. In most of the offices the floors were bare boards and the walls were posted with wanted flyers. Few of the offices had curtains, and their furnishings were plain as well as being scarred and battered from hard use.

This office resembled a small neat parlor. A Brussels carpet covered the floor. On a round mahogany table gleaming with polish a double-globe oil lamp shed a mellow glow. A upholstered damask sofa stood against one wall, faced by a pair of velvet-cushioned easy chairs. Behind the chairs there was a small rolltop desk, flanked incongrously by a gun rack of gleaming brazilwood. The rack held three rifles and two shotguns, their blue steel barrels and bird's-eye maple stocks glistening in the light shed by the lamp. Beyond it a clothes rack held a neatly checked blue coat.

Longarm's amazement did not interfere with his quick scrutiny of the man seated in one of the chairs. The man was not large. The chair he occupied dwarfed his modestly sized frame. He had on a vest and trousers which matched the coat on the clothes rack. His beard was neatly trimmed, but his mustache had been given full rein to grow and it hid his mouth completely. He turned to look at Longarm with pale blue ice-cold eyes.

"Are you looking for someone?" he asked. "Is there some sort of trouble that brings you here?"

"Well, I take it you're Commodore Owens, the sheriff here, so you'd be the man I'm looking for. My name's Long, Custis Long, deputy United States marshal outta the Denver office."

"If you're the one they call Longarm, I'm acquainted with your reputation," Owens said. "I take it this is just a friendly visit? Or perhaps I should say fraternal."

"Well, I never shy away from a lawman, especially when I'm on a case, which is why I'm here, Commodore Owens. I figured I better stop in and get acquainted, because I might need to call on you for some information now and then."

"My full name is Commodore Perry Owens," the man said. "And you're correct in assuming that I'm the sheriff. But as for your case, while I suppose that I should welcome you here, I must warn you at the beginning that I do not look favorably on outside lawmen invading my jurisdiction."

# Chapter 11

Longarm stood speechless for a moment. At last he said, "Well, now, Sheriff Commodore Perry Owens, I'm sorry to hear you say that, but I guess I got to give you credit for getting down to brass tacks right at the start."

"I'm not trying to make you feel unwelcome, Marshal Long," Owens went on. "However, I'm sure you're familiar with the old saying about too many cooks spoiling the broth."

"Sure. But I remember that there's another old saying about the barrel telling the box two heads is better than one. Now, I don't mess into another lawman's cases any more'n I'd want somebody poking their noses into mine. And I won't make no extra trouble for you if I can help it, but this case that's brought me here is one that I got what you'd call a real personal interest in closing."

"Perhaps you'd better explain what you mean by personal interest," Owens suggested. "I try to keep my attitude toward every case totally impersonal."

"I ain't going to argue that with you. But if you're like me, it gets to be right-down personal sometimes. Like when it's a case where the crook you're after has sent a hired killer to cut you down without no reason except he figures his man's got a chance to get you before you catch up with him."

For a moment the sheriff was silent, then he nodded. "Yes, I suppose that would be a personal interest. It just happens that since I've put on my badge I've never been in the situation you describe. But I gather that you've had more experience as a lawman than I have."

"Now, that don't rightly follow," Longarm said. "It ain't always how long you've been a lawman that counts when the chips are down. All I'm even pretty sure about is there was a hired killer here in Holbrook who had a bullet with my name on it his gun."

"And the man who hired the killer? He also lived here in Holbrook?"

A rueful frown formed on Longarm's face. He shook his head slowly. "I can't say yes and I can't say no to that one, Sheriff. Not yet, at least. And it just might be that I've come here on what a lot of lawmen'd likely call a damnfool hunch."

"I'd say it's quite a long trip for you to take if it's only the result of guesswork," Owens told him.

"Oh, you ain't heard the whole story yet," Longarm said quickly. "And it's a mite crossed up too. About all I can say is, it makes sense to me."

"I can understand that I'm not in a position to judge until I know more about this case of yours. Suppose you sit down and tell me a bit more. You'll find that chair you're standing beside is quite comfortable."

"Well, now," Longarm began after he'd settled into the chair. "You might say I been sorta jumping from pillar to post lately. What I been doing is trying to find a man that sent a hired killer from here in Holbrook all the way to Denver to cut me down. And I got to admit before you get around to asking, I don't have no idea why he sent a gunhand after me. But I guess you've seen cases like that yourself, Commodore Perry?"

"To be truthful, I haven't," the Gila County sheriff confessed. "But this job's still somewhat new to me. Go ahead and tell me about your case, Marshal Long."

"I don't expect you'd mind if I light a cigar first?" Longarm asked.

Owens shook his head, and Longarm touched a match to one of his long thin cheroots. He puffed at it until the tip was glowing to his satisfaction, then began recounting the pertinent portions of his his experiences and travels. His narration began with the attack of the hired gunman in Denver and the gunfight that he and Billy Vail had had with the would-be assassin. Then he jumped to his futile efforts to trace the man after reaching Arizona Territory. The Gila County sheriff listened in attentive silence until Longarm reached the point of his experience in the Phoenix bank and mentioned the name Redford Trent.

"Hold on a minute," Owens interrupted. "As well as I can remember, there's no one by that name here in Holbrook."

"Are you certain sure of that?" Longarm asked.

"Holbrook's a small town, Marshal Long. It's one of those places where everybody knows everybody else," Owens replied. "When I first moved here it took me about a week to learn not just their names, but what their jobs are, the names of their relatives, and what all of them are doing." -

"Now, that ain't what I had in mind," Longarm protested. "But I got—"

As though Longarm had not interrupted him, Owens kept talking and Longarm fell silent again. "Don't you believe for a minute that I'm the kind of sheriff who sits in his office all the time," the sheriff went on. "I go out and visit with people and talk to them every day. I'd say you've been a lawman long enough to know that when I've got to call on men to join a posse, I need to be sure I get the ones I can depend on instead of some who'll turn tail and run."

Longarm nodded. "I know just what you're talking about, Sheriff. But that wasn't in my mind either. I was just surprised a mite when you told me you didn't know of nobody here in town named Trent. Do you figure he might be a hand on one of the ranches hereabouts?"

"I know every hand on every ranch in Gila County!" Owens insisted. "They're on my visiting list too. When those men come to town on their payday toot, I know which ones are going to behave and which ones are likely to give me some trouble."

Longarm was quick to ask, "Then how are you going to get around what I found out at that bank in Phoenix, where this Redford Trent's account is? The big boss at that place got Trent's town right off the bank's list of customers."

"Oh, I don't doubt for a minute what you've told me about somebody who lives here using that name at the post office here," Owens assured him. "And in a town this size, all we've got to do is find out who it is."

"You think maybe the postmaster or one of the clerks at the post office will know?"

"As I've mentioned before, Holbrook's a small town, Marshal Long. It's not like your home station in Denver. There aren't any clerks at the post office here. The postmaster himself does all the work."

"And I'd guess it's a little bit late in the day to be calling on him?"

Owens shook his head. "No, it's not all that late. Usually, I'd just take you to his house. But when I was in the post office today, talking to Bob Little— that's the postmaster—he mentioned that he'd be taking his wife out to her cousin's ranch to have supper and spend the night. By this time they've already left to go out there. But surely you can wait until tomorrow to get the information you're after?"

"Well, I don't put up no argument when there's nobody's mind to change. And I don't reckon there's all that much of a hurry, Sheriff Owens," Longarm said as he stood up. "Now, I guess you've had a pretty long day, just like I have. I'll leave you to finish up your own work and go find me a place where I can grab a handful of shut-eye."

"Try the Holbrook House," Owens suggested. "It's run by a widow woman, Mrs. Carrie Hill. Just go left when you leave and take the second turn left, you'll see her sign. Her place might be full, but if you tell her I sent you she'll make room for you somehow."

"Now, that's what I'd call funny—not funny to laugh about, but sorta odd. On the way to your office here, I stopped to wash the trail dust outta my throat with a swallow of rye whiskey and the barkeep told me I'd be likely to find a good clean room at Miz Hill's place."

"Everybody in town knows she keeps a good boarding-house, and everybody likes her," the sheriff said. "I'll be looking for you in the morning, and we'll go see the postmaster."

When Longarm stepped out of the sheriff's office, darkness had settled in completely, and a quick glance at the few lights that still glowed from the town's main street told him that most of Holbrook's citizens had settled in for the night. He swung into his saddle and reined his horse past the glowing pinpoints of brightness.

Reaching the second intersection, where Owens had told him to turn, Longarm hesitated for a moment, his eyes fixed on the main street that ran through Holbrook. He was sure he'd find a saloon open ahead where he could have a nightcap, but after a moment's thought he shook his head.

"Old son," Longarm said aloud as he reined his horse into the intersecting street, "a nightcap'd go down real fine right now, but what you need more'n that is a bed. So just show some sense for once and do what know you ought to instead of what you'd just like to."

After his mount had taken him past two cross streets Longarm saw the sign Owens had described and pulled up. A lighted lantern hung from the eaves above the porch of the house where he'd stopped, and lamplight glowed through curtains at one of the windows beside the door. Dismounting, he stepped up to the porch and tapped on the door. He'd barely had time to let his hand fall after knocking when the door opened and a woman stepped to the porch.

"Evening, ma'am," he said. "I reckon you'd be Miz Carrie Hill? Because if you are, from what I was told in town, you rent out rooms."

"I'm Carrie Hill and you were told right," she answered. "I rent by the day, week, or month." She was flicking her eyes over Longarm's travel-stained clothing as she talked. "I'd say you sure look like you're ready for a place to stop."

"I am that," he said. "There was a fellow I run into right after I got here that told me about your boardinghouse, and so did the sheriff. That's why I come here."

"If Sheriff Owens sent you, I don't reckon I need to worry," she told him. "Because I don't rent my rooms to every Tom, Dick, and Harry that comes knocking at my door."

"You don't need to worry a bit, ma'am," Longarm told her. "I'm a deputy United States marshal. My name's Custis Long."

"Pleased to know you, Marshal Long," she said. "And if the men you talked to didn't mention what I charge, it's fifty cents for a room for the night. But when folks stay a week or more, it's worth it to me to give them a rate of two dollars and a half. If they stay longer, I take off an extra nickel a day. Baths are twenty cents, and I'll lend you a towel. But I don't serve meals at all, not even breakfast."

"I could sure use a bath before I go to bed," Longarm told her. "If it wouldn't put you to a lot of trouble. And I might be here a while, maybe even longer than a week, so if it's all right with you, I'll just pay the two dollars and a half, then square up with you for whatever baths I take before I leave."

"That'll suit me fine," she said. "And if that's your horse out by the street, you can lead him around back where there's a little place I've got fenced in for horses and my cow. I guess you can find it all right in the dark?"

"More'n half the time my work's done in the dark, ma'am," Longarm told her. "It won't faze me a bit to get the horse unsaddled and give him a little fodder."

"Generally, I don't feed horses, but there's always some leftover hay back there. And there's a livery right up the street where you can feed him in the morning. Just leave your saddle gear on the back stoop tonight."

While they'd been talking, Longarm had been sizing up the landlady. In the dim light it was difficult for him to decide about her age. All that he could make out was that Carrie Hill had high cheekbones, a small uptilted nose, and a firm chin. Her eyes were dark and her lips full. He guessed that she might have passed her middle forties. Her face was rounded, and moderate wrinkles showed at the ends of her eyes and the corners of her mouth, but her neck was shadowed between her jawline and the high collar of her dress.

"Well, now," he said. "Suppose I lead my horse around back and get my saddle off of him. Then when I come inside, we'll square up the rent and all."

"You go ahead with your chores," she said. "I'll open the door to your room so you won't have any trouble finding it. Just come in the back way and walk right up the hall. I'll tap on your door after I figure you've had time to settle in."

Longarm went back to his horse and led the animal around the house. There was no moon, but the starlight of the high desert country was a more than adequate substitute for moonlight.

He made short work of unsaddling, and when he'd finished he stepped to the door of the shed to see if there was enough hay in the trough to give the animal a feeding. He struck a match to find the feed-rack, saw that it held enough fodder to satisfy his mount, and blew out the match before scooping up an armful of hay with his free hand.

Dropping the hay in the miniature corral outside the barn, Longarm picked up his saddle gear and rifle and deposited the saddle on the small back porch. Pulling his Winchester from its scabbard, he went in the back door and gazed up the long hall. A glow of lamplight was coming from an open door near the entry and he started toward it. Just before he reached it, Carrie Hill stepped out of the door into the hall.

"You mentioned you'd want a bath, Marshal Long," she said. "And I happened to have a kettle of hot water on the stove, so I emptied it in the tub. There's another kettle full of cold on the floor there. You can just pour in as much as you need. And your room's all ready."

"Well, I sure do thank you, ma'am," Longarm told her. "Now, if you want me to pay my rent—"

"That can wait till morning," she told him. "You're trail-tired, and I figure you're good for the rent, seeing as you're a lawman."

"Whatever suits you, suits me," Longarm replied.

"Tomorrow'll be fine then," she answered. "I'll leave you now and let you get to your bath before the water cools."

She turned to go, and Longarm glanced into the bathroom. The water in the tub was glistening invitingly in the lamplight. He hurried to his room, stripped to his underwear, and pulled his spare underwear from his saddlebag.

Although he was sure that he'd be undisturbed by other guests at such a late hour, he took his usual precaution of lifting his Colt from its holster and carrying it with him as he stepped into the corridor. He left the door unlocked, and took the two quick steps down the hallway to the bathroom.

Shucking off his sweat-stained underwear, Longarm wasted no time emptying the pail of hot water into the tub and stepping in. The water was only lukewarm, but its small warmth was relaxingly welcome. A bar of soap was in a dish on the floor beside the tub. Lowering himself into the water, he picked up the soap, made a short job of lathering himself, and rinsed away the suds. Then for a few minutes he lay back as the warm water eased muscles that had been used to the full on his long horseback ride from Phoenix and during the skirmish with the Apaches.

Gradually, the already tepid water cooled. After a final rinse, Longarm stood up and toweled quickly. He picked up his fresh underwear and started to step into it. He'd lifted one foot before he realized that he would be shedding the underwear for bed almost at once.

Draping both suits of underwear over his shoulder, he cracked open the door leading into the hall. The night-light at the rear of the passageway was glowing dimly, but was bright enough to show him that the corridor was deserted. Longarm moved quickly to the door of his room, and opened it just widely enough to step backward into the chamber. He locked the door, and with the click of the latch-bolt he turned toward the bed.

"I thought you'd be a careful man," Carrie Hill said as she sat up in the bed, allowing the coverlet to slide away from her bare shoulders. "And I'm glad to see that I was right. Now that we know we won't be disturbed, why don't you put your pistol down and join me?"

For a moment, Longarm could only stare speechless. Recovering quickly from his first amazed glance, he said, "I got to admit I wasn't expecting to see nobody in here, so you sorta took me by surprise. I don't guess there's many boardinghouses where the landlady makes a new boarder all this welcome."

"I'd say you're right about that," she told him. "And I don't do it myself very often, but a widow-woman who's been used to having a husband handy gets the same kind of itch a man does."

"Well, I ain't the kind that makes a lady ask twice," Longarm went on. "So I'm just going to take your invitation."

"I was sure you would," she told him as she threw back the bedclothes.

Without taking his eyes off Carrie and the neatly contoured body she'd uncovered, Longarm shrugged to rid himself of the underwear draped over his shoulder. He stepped to the bed and laid his Colt on the floor beside it, then stood for a moment glancing down at his unexpected guest.

Carrie was propped up on her elbows now, raising her shoulders, her figure fully revealed. Longarm swept his eyes from her upraised face to her bulgingly full pink-tipped breasts which sagged only slightly. Her stomach was a very small mound broken by the dimple of her navel, her dark pubic bush small and thin. Her thighs were well-rounded, and as Carrie saw Longarm's gaze shifting she spread them invitingly, and lifted her knees.

Longarm had reached a full erection during the few moments spent scanning his unexpected guest's inviting form. He bent and kneeled on the side of the bed. Carrie

141

spread her thighs to accept him, and shifted her hips slightly to roll toward him, dropping one leg as Longarm moved above her. She placed him quickly and Longarm thrust.

"Ohh!" she sighed as she brought up her hips to meet his lunge. "I knew the minute I laid eyes on you that you'd be the sort of man who knows how to please a woman! Now hump, and keep on driving till I have to beg you to stop!"

After the long and lonely days of traveling by himself through country where one seldom saw a human face, Longarm was more than willing to oblige. He drove with slow and measured strokes for several minutes, while Carrie rocked and brought her hips up to meet his lusty strokes. When Longarm felt himself building too swiftly, or when Carrie began writhing her hips and twisting her torso too enthusiastically and out of rhythm with his steady thrusts, he stopped for a minute or so to delay the onset of her climax, holding himself buried deeply while she revolved her buttocks and sighed with gusty moans.

Often when she was wriggling and heaving up her hips in one of her ultimate responses to Longarm's deep lunges, Carrie offered him her lips, and both of them remained motionless for a few moments, easing their urgency as their tongues met in moist caresses. Then without any signal from either of them, Longarm resumed his steady rhythmic driving until the next time their instincts warned them to stop if they wanted their pleasures to be prolonged.

Inevitably, the moment came when neither of the happenstance lovers could find the willpower to stop as the moment of climax grew close. They shuddered and sighed while Longarm held himself pressed against her, lips glued together until their spasmic shudders faded and came to an end. At last Carrie turned her head to break their kiss.

"I don't think I can go much more," she whispered.

"Maybe just this one more time," Longarm urged.

He was beginning a fresh lunge as he spoke. He stepped up the tempo of his driving, and as his thrusts became stronger Carrie squirmed each time their bodies thwacked together. A moan deeper in pitch than those she'd been releasing ebbed from her lips. Longarm closed them with his own lips, and as their tongues twined again he drove to their climax. The reflexive quivering of their bodies ebbed slowly, and finally stopped.

For several minutes they lay motionless. Then Carrie whispered, "I think I'd better go back to my room now. But you're going to be here another night or two, when we can get started earlier."

"And I'll be waiting till the next time," Longarm promised.

Pressing a quick kiss on his lips, Carrie got out of bed, grabbed her dress from the chair beside the bed, and slipped out the door. Longarm did not bother to get up and lock it. He turned on his side, punched the pillow several times to fluff it up, and closed his eyes. In less than a minute he was asleep.

# Chapter 12

As pleasantly satisfying as Longarm's night with Carrie
Hill had been, it had also been long and exhausting.
Though he'd been tempted to remain in bed when he
first woke up and blinked his eyes at the light lines of
pre-dawn gray trickling into his room around the edges
of the window shade, Longarm rolled out of bed. Only
minutes later he had dressed and was saddling his horse.
By the time he reached the center of Holbrook, the gray
of the eastern sky was tinged with pink.

Longarm was not surprised to see lamplight glowing
above and below the swinging doors of the saloon where
he'd stopped for a drink the evening before. He knew that
even in small Western towns that were located at important trail junctions, most saloons stayed open around the
clock. He was only mildly surprised when he pushed
through the batwings and found the barroom was totally
deserted except for the lone barkeeper who was standing
with his back to the door, busy polishing glasses at the
back bar.

He was both surprised and pleased when the man behind the bar turned, for now Longarm recognized him as Benjamin Franklin Stewart, who'd been so helpful with advice on his earlier visit. Even before he'd crossed the sawdust-strewn floor floor to the back bar, the young barkeep had placed the bottle of rye whiskey and a glass on the freshly wiped mahogany to be ready for Longarm when he stopped at the bar.

"I wasn't really expecting to see you again so soon, friend," Stewart said, indicating the bottle and glass with a gesture of his hand. "Especially after you being in here so late yesterday. But I figured you'd want the same whiskey you had before."

"And you figured right," Longarm said. "A man in my line of work don't get much chance to sleep in of a morning." He dropped a cartwheel on the bar and picked up the bottle of whiskey. "When I'm back on my home grounds, I keep a bottle of rye handy in my room so I can have a wake-up sip while I'm getting my clothes on."

"If you don't mind me showing my curiosity, where might your home grounds be?"

"Why, I work outta Denver," Longarm replied. "And I don't guess I mentioned my name last night when we was talking about names and you was polite enough to tell me that yours is Benjamin Franklin Stewart. Folks call you Ben, you said?"

"Mostly," Stewart said. "I'm not like Sheriff Owens."

"Well, mine's Long, Custis Long." Longarm was filling his glass as he spoke. "Now if you're ready for an early drink, Ben, I'd sure be pleased to stand you one."

"I appreciate the offer, and I hope your feelings won't be hurt if I pass again."

"Not one bit," Longarm assured him. "Like Miz O'Leary said when she kissed the cow, everybody to their own taste."

"I'd like nothing better than to join you," the young bartender told him. "But I'm not ashamed any longer when I own up to being one of those fellows who can't stop tossing down liquor after they've had a drink or two. After I'd watched them get falling-down drunk night after night, and just missed falling down with 'em a few times, I made up my mind that I'd be better off if I turned teetotaler, so I did."

"At least you got enough sense to do what you seen you ought to do," Longarm told him. "And enough sand in your craw to do it." As he spoke he lighted one of his long thin cigars. He puffed and exhaled, then tossed off the liquor.

"Next drink's on the house," Stewart said, reaching for the bottle of rye.

Longarm shook his head. "Thanks, Ben, but no thanks. One's all I take of a morning. It sorta helps pop my eyes open."

"I guess you found a place to stay last night?" the barman asked.

"I sure did. Went right where you told me to. It's funny, but Sheriff Owens said the same things about that boarding house as you did."

"Everybody around here tries to help Miz Carrie," Stewart explained. "And from what you just said, I gather that you found the sheriff without any trouble?"

"He was just where you said he'd be," Longarm said. "So we had our little talk. I'm just waiting for it to get a bit later before I go back and visit with him again."

"You know, I sort of figured you to be a lawman after you asked about the sheriff when you stopped in last night," Ben said. "Was I guessing right?"

"You sure was. I'm a deputy United States marshal."

"Well, there's times now and then when I wish I was doing the same kind of work you are," Ben said. "My daddy didn't want me to be a lawman, though. He wanted me to be a cowboy like he was before he got crippled up in a stampede and set up this saloon. Then he died and left it to me, and—well, I just keep on running it."

"Your family's been around here a long time then?"

"Quite a spell. My daddy came out here to work on the Hashknife when they bought up all the little spreads up above the Mogollon Rim. Holbrook was just a couple of crossroads stores and a few shacks then, so without stretching the truth I guess you can say I saw it grow up."

"I reckon you'd know most of the folks hereabouts?"

"Most of 'em, I suppose," Ben answered. "Maybe not some of the Johnny-come-latelies, of course."

"Did you ever happen to hear of a fellow in Holbrook named Redford Trent?"

For a moment the young saloon man looked thoughtful. Then he shook his head. "I can't say I have. I guess he'd be somebody you're looking for here in town?"

"You guessed right," Longarm answered. "Except that when I mentioned his name to Sheriff Owens, he'd never heard of him. But from the way I understand things, Sheriff Owens hasn't lived here as long as you have."

"Most folks haven't, and there've been a lot of new people come here since the railroad was put in. And you're right about the sheriff not having been here long. He was running a little horse ranch up at Navajo Springs,

148

and doing pretty well, from what I've heard. Then all of a sudden he got the bug to be sheriff. So he put his name on the ballot, and got elected."

"And what kinda sheriff's he been?"

"A right good one. But nobody's had the spunk to go against him since he cleaned up the Blevins gang."

"That's one I've never heard about," Longarm said. "How big of a gang was it?"

"I don't guess nobody but the Blevinses really knows how many there was in the bunch, but there was four of them in that gunfight I mentioned. All four of 'em was in the house they'd been using for a hideout here in town, and Sheriff Owens was outside. From what I heard, the outlaws fired the first shot, then Sheriff Owens started shooting. He killed three and never got a scratch. All of a sudden, there wasn't a Blevins gang any longer, nor any other ones right here around Holbrook."

"And I don't imagine any new gang's got started since then?" Longarm asked.

"Not so's you'd notice."

"Well, it's good to know that your sheriff's a man a fellow can tie to," Longarm said. "And speaking of the sheriff, I guess we been palavering long enough to give him time to get to his office, so I better be moseying on down there."

Holbrook was just beginning to wake up as Longarm mounted his horse and let it pick its own gait up the hard-packed yellow soil of the street that led to the sheriff's office. In most of the business buildings he passed men in citified suits were standing in the doorways, awaiting the day's early customers. There were few people on the street, and those who were visible all seemed to be in a hurry to get somewhere.

Longarm reached the small building that housed the sheriff's office. Commodore Perry Owens was standing at a corner of the little structure. His head was bent over a revolver, his hands busy trying to perform some sort of operation which Longarm could not quite make out. Owens looked up and nodded.

"Good morning, Marshal Long," he called.

"Morning, Sheriff Owens," Longarm greeted him. He dismounted, looped the reins of his horse around the hitch rail, and started walking toward the sheriff as he added, "You know, I got a sorta nickname that most folks I'm friends with call me by. It's Longarm."

"I've heard it mentioned more than once since I've been sheriff," Owens said. "You prefer it to your real name, I suppose?"

"Well, now, I don't care much one way or the other, but I'm used to it." Longarm had reached Perry's side by now. "Looks like you're having a mite of trouble with that pistol of yours."

"More than a mite," Owens replied. "It's a stubborn weapon, but if it worked right, I'd certainly be satisfied to carry it in my holster."

Longarm looked at the revolver and frowned. "Where in blazes did you find that thing, Sheriff? Ain't it one of them old Navy pistols? Seems to me they was made by some outfit called Walks or Walts, something like that."

"You're right about the pistol, but a little bit off on the name," Owens replied. "It's a Walch revolver, .45-caliber. Since you recognized it so quickly, I suppose you know that this gun's supposed to fire twelve shots without reloading."

"You're right as rain," Longarm agreed. "I run across one of them guns something like ten years ago. After I'd

150

bought it, I found out that it didn't do like it ought to. It kept on hanging up and quitting after I'd let off about four or five rounds, generally just about the time I'd be needing it most."

"I've found out the same thing, Longarm," Owens replied. "I got it off a dead Apache something like three or four years ago, and ever since then I've been trying to find a way to modify the action to make it work all the time."

"Well, I sure wish you luck," Longarm told him. "And I don't mean to butt in on what you're doing, but if you got the time to leave your office for a little spell, I'm as ready as I'll ever be to go to your post office here and see what I can find out about this Redford Trent fellow."

"I suppose the sooner we start, the faster we'll know," Owens agreed. He let the hand holding the revolver drop to his side and started for the office door. "I've been thinking a bit about this case that's brought you here, but I can't make too much sense out of it."

"You know, Sheriff, I've found out there's times when a lawman don't think like the scoundrel he's after," Longarm said. "But I got to admit it's a mite hard to figure out what some crook might have in mind when you ain't even got a hint about who you're after might be."

"Do you happen to have any hints you didn't think to mention when we were talking yesterday?"

Longarm shook his head. "Nary a one."

"I haven't either," Owens confessed. "I've been trying to recall whether I've run across anybody named Trent who lives in town here, or perhaps one of the ranches close by, but I'll admit I haven't been able to."

They were in the sheriff's office now. Owens put the Walch revolver in a battered box that stood on his desk and strapped on his gunbelt. Longarm noted that the belt supported two .45 Colt revolvers, but decided not to comment on the sheriff being a two-gun man. He stood watching while Owens slid his arms into his coat sleeves and shrugged the coat on, pulled it into place, and reached for his black derby hat.

"Whenever you're ready, Marshal—Longarm," he said. "If we leave right now, we'll get to the post office just about the time Bob Little's unlocking the front door."

"This Bob Little, he'd be the postmaster?" Longarm asked as he and Owens went out the office door and started toward the hitch rail.

Owens nodded. "Bob's been postmaster here about two years. Fine young man, and Holbrook certainly needed a young one from what I've heard. Old Jim Allen had the job from the time Holbrook was big enough to have a post office, but he finally decided to step down."

"I reckon he'd still be around town, though?" Longarm asked. "Because it seems like I've heard that name before, except that right this minute I can't quite recall where or when it was."

"Allen's not an uncommon name," Owens said. "It's possible that you might've run into him somewhere before he got the job here. He'd been postmaster of two or three big offices in other places before he got sent here to start this one up. From what I've heard, he was transferred here because he was getting too old to hold down his previous job. It seems that he'd gotten cranky with the people who'd come into the post office and—well, just generally hard to get along with."

"I don't reckon it's all that important whether I've run into him before," Longarm said. "Except that if he put in a pretty good spell here, he might know about this Redford Trent that sent a hired gun all the way to Denver to cut me down."

As Longarm and Owens talked they'd let their mounts set their own easy pace on the road toward the post office. Although it was still early in the day, there were more people on the move along the street than Longarm had noticed before. Most of them were on foot, but wagons and a few buggies as well as a number of saddle horses were hitched to the rails in front of the saloons and stores.

Owens gestured ahead as he said, "I don't know whether you've noticed where our post office is, but that's it over to the right, next to the big general store."

"To tell you the truth, I hadn't," Longarm replied as his eyes followed the sheriff's gesture. "I guess we better rein over and hitch up as close as we can, because there ain't a bare spot I can see at the rails right in front of the post office."

"There's always a crowd in the post office at this time of the morning," Owens told him. "But I've worked out a way with Bob Little to save me a lot of waiting time. I just step inside and take a look around. If there are too many people lined up at the window, I give Bob a wave, then he opens the back door and hands me my mail."

They'd gone a short distance past the post office and reached a spot where there was space at a hitch rail for both of their horses. After they'd pulled up the animals and looped the reins over the rail, the sheriff started for a gap between the post-office building and the general-merchandise store adjoining it.

"I reckon you know that getting your mail like you do ain't according to what the post office rules says," Longarm remarked, his voice carefully casual. "Not that I'm always of a mind to agree with 'em, but their rules book says there ain't supposed to be nobody but the men that works at the post office in the places where they do the sorting and all like that."

"Nobody's ever mentioned that me," Owens said. "Damn it, I'm an officer of the law just like you are, and we ought to be bound by the law, not breaking it!"

"Why, I just said what I did to josh you a little bit, Sheriff Owens." Longarm smiled. "There's times when a lawman's got to bend some of the damn-fool rules that them pencil-pushers and clerks back in Washington make up. I just happen to know about that post office rule because us Federal marshals is supposed to learn what's right and wrong for every one of the government's departments. And that takes in a lot of territory."

"You mean you know all the rules for the post office and the land office and the navy and War Department and Attorney General's office and all the rest of them?" the sheriff asked.

"Well, now, I wouldn't go so far as to say I know all of 'em by heart," Longarm replied. "And just between you and me and the gatepost, when I get into some sorta fracas where all the chips is on the table and I got to bend one of them rules, I do it."

Owens nodded. "I see that you and I have the same ideas about some things."

"That's about the size of it," Longarm agreed.

They'd reached the back door of the post office by now. Owens tapped on it, three quick raps followed by three more. A moment or two passed. Then there was the click of a lock being turned. The door opened a crack and a man's eyes peered through the slit between the door and jamb.

"I guess I ought've known it was you, Sheriff," he said, opening the door. "You and the railroad baggage-handler that brings the mailbags from the depot are the only ones that knock at this door. But I don't recognize the gentleman with you."

Before Owens could reply, Longarm said, extending his hand, "My name's Long, Custis Long. I work for the government, same as you do. I'm a deputy U.S. marshal outta the Denver office. If you want to see my badge—"

"There's no need to show it," the man replied, taking Longarm's hand and gripping it for a moment. He swung the door open as he went on. "Commodore Perry wouldn't bring you here with him unless he knew for sure that you're who you say you are. Come right in. I'll be with you just as soon as I get to the end of the line at the General Delivery window."

Owens gestured for Longarm to go in first, then followed him into the room. The postmaster hurried back to the service window and started a conversation at once with whoever was waiting in the post office lobby. Longarm used the opportunity to scan his new surroundings.

A window on each side of the room let the morning light stream in, though neither of them caught the sunlight. The back wall was broken only by the door through which Longarm and Owens had entered. Centered in the front wall was the latticed window where the postmaster was now standing. The remainder of the wall was covered by the post office boxes, a latticework of small open

155

rectangles, most of them with the ends of envelopes protruding. A rolltop desk stood on one side of the rear door, and a small table on the other. The desk was closed, the table strewn with neat stacks of letters.

Dominating the room was a large square table with U-shaped openings on all four sides. Its surface was quite literally covered with small boxes and bundles and neat stacks of envelopes and postcards.

"It looks like your friend Little keeps a real neat shop," Longarm commented. "It ain't that I know all that much about how a post office is supposed to look, but it seems all right to me."

"It's a big improvement over the way it looked when old Jim Allen was postmaster," Owens said. "I was in here a time or two before the department retired him, and while I'm not any expert on post offices, this room was a mess. Mailbags all over the place that never seemed to get opened, always a lot of the mail scattered around on the floor where that big table is, things of that sort. And toward the last, before the higher-ups in Washington retired Jim, I'd say it got worse."

As Owens stopped speaking, Bob Little turned away from the lobby window and stepped up to join them. He asked Longarm, "Are you here on official business, Marshal Long? Or is this just a courtesy call?"

"Oh, I'm on a case," Longarm replied. "And before you get busy at that window again, I better tell you about it."

"A criminal case?" Little asked. "I'm not questioning your authority, Marshal Long, but I'm surprised. I'm sure you know that our own department's inspectors handle any crimes connected with the postal service."

"Sure," Longarm replied. "But this case started back in Denver, which is the office I work out of. I'll tell you about all the ins and outs of it soon as you've got the time, maybe when you close up this evening. But right now I need to know just one thing, and that's where I might be able to find out who's got the key to your post office box number seventeen."

"That shouldn't be difficult," Little said. He went to the desk and took out a box crammed with cards placed on edge. He brought it back to where Longarm and Owens waited. "This is our master file," he explained. "It's indexed by name and address and our post office box number, and it's supposed to list everybody here in Holbrook as well as our rural routes. I'm sure . . ."

Little broke off suddenly and glanced at the open backs of the cubbyholes that filled the front wall of the big bare room. Most of them had envelopes or magazines or newspapers sticking out of their open backs. "Now, that's odd," Little went on. "Just before the morning rush started about thirty minutes ago, I put two large envelopes in box seventeen. Now it's empty!"

# Chapter 13

"You sure about that?" Longarm asked the postmaster.

"As sure as I am that the three of us are standing here talking," the postmaster said. "There was one envelope in that box, it'd been there for three or four days. I put two more in—well, maybe an hour to an hour and a half ago."

"It was letters you put in, I guess?" Longarm asked.

"Of course," Little replied. "And now that I've begun thinking about them, I remember glancing at them, maybe because I noticed they were both from a bank. It was the same bank, and the postmark showed they'd been mailed at the same time. I recall wondering why they'd wasted an extra stamp by not putting both of them in one envelope."

"You don't recall the name of the bank then?" Longarm asked. "Or where the stamp showed it was mailed?"

Little shook his head as he replied, "I just plain don't remember even noticing it. I guess it's likely I've handled the same kind of envelopes before, Marshal Long, but—

well, I'm really not sure why, but I guess you and Sheriff Owens both know there are some things that just get buried away in a man's head without much rhyme or reason and you can't seem to dig 'em out."

By this time Longarm had decided it was going to be necessary to lead the postmaster by jogging his memory. "Oh, sure," he agreed. "But this bank, now. Could it've been the Security Bank of Arizona?"

"That's it! And the postmark was Phoenix!" Little was almost shouting. "I'm sorry I was so forgetful, Marshal Long. I don't know why I didn't remember right off. I guess it's because I look at so much mail while I'm sorting it that I don't give it much notice when I'm stuffing it in the boxes and pigeonholes. Either that, or my memory gets a little bit quirky when it comes to carrying names in mind."

"I'm sure that Longarm and I both understand that," Owens said. "But you were talking about your master file."

"Of course," the postmaster replied. He referred to the box filled with small cards. "If I don't have that name in here, I'll be the most surprised man in Arizona Territory."

While he was talking, Little had started running his fingers along the tops of the cards in the file. He selected one and as he slid it out he said, "Here it is. Box seventeen." Lifting out the card, Little glanced at it, then raised his head and shook it slowly from side to side as a puzzled frown puckered his brow. He went on. "I'm afraid I spoke too soon. The card's blank. There's no name on it. The only thing written on it is the box number."

"How in tunket could that happen?" Longarm asked. "I seem to recall that a while back, when I was on a case when I had to run down some letters at the post office, one of your inspectors told me the rules said the postmaster had to keep a list of the names of folks that rented boxes."

"Your memory's good, Marshal Long," Little told him. "And I guess I'll never know how I missed noticing this blank card when I was working with Jim Allen while I was fixing to take over the office here, and going over all his books and records. Damn it, postal regulations are strict! This isn't the sort of thing I'd overlook!"

"Well, I can see that," Longarm said. "But it'd seem like—"

"Just a minute, Longarm," Sheriff Owens said. He turned to Little and asked, "You're sure Jim was with you all the time? Because he should've noticed—or maybe I'd better say that he should've *known* that card was blank. He was in charge here for a long time, and he certainly couldn't've missed knowing about it."

"Now, that was just about the same thing I was going to mention," Longarm said. "And that don't mean but one thing to me. If he put that blank card in there, and pulled it out before he left his job after you took over, he'd've had to have a reason for doing it."

"You're suggesting that Jim Allen was mixed up in some sort of underhanded goings-on?" Little frowned. "He never did strike me as being the sort of man you're suggesting he might be."

"Well, the way it looks right now, that's about all I can think of," Longarm replied. "And since it's starting to look like there might've been some kinda connection between him and all that money I found out about being tucked away in that Phoenix bank, I aim to have a word with him."

"Now?" Owens frowned.

"If we don't do it now, all we'd be doing is spinning our wheels like a locomotive that's just run through a hog herd on the tracks," Longarm told the sheriff. "I reckon you know where this Allen fellow lives?"

"Of course," Owens replied. "He's got a little house about a half mile north of here, along one of the trails that used to be handy to town before the railroad line was built across it. The railroad track gangs closed off all but two or three trails, put big log barricades between them and the tracks. That was when they were laying rail a few years back, but it didn't seem to bother Allen."

"Then I guess I better go out there right now and have a little visit with this Jim Allen," Longarm said. "And it'll save me a lot of time looking if you'll do me the favor of going along to show me the trail or road out there, if there is one. You know just where to find the place, and soon as you set me right on how to get to it, you can come back and take care of your regular business."

"Why, I certainly don't begrudge any time I spend giving you what help I can, Longarm," the sheriff replied. "But it's your case, and I don't want to get in your way."

"I wouldn't be asking for help if I didn't feel like I need it," Longarm told Owens. "But I ain't going to eat away at time you need for your own job. Just ride out with me to where that crossing used to be. I'll find my own way from there. Then I can come back here and ask Postmaster Little whatever else I might need to know without using up any more of your time."

Owens smiled. "Well, there are a few things I need to tend to before the day gets too far along. If you're ready to ride, I'm right with you."

• • •

Longarm touched a lighted match to his long thin cigar, and as its tip started glowing he twisted in his saddle for a final glance over his shoulder at Owens. The sheriff was already heading back to Holbrook after showing Longarm the starting point of the broken trail that wound across the barren land beyond the spot where it crossed the railroad tracks. Between Longarm's position and the level desert land beyond the rails only small sections of the trail were visible, for the scatterings of loose dirt tossed by the shovels of grading crews covered most of the downslope beyond the level shelf cut for the rails.

On the way to the tracks neither Longarm nor Owens had felt the need for commenting on the dead end they'd encountered at the post office. After the sheriff had indicated the starting point of the trail they'd exchanged nods, Longarm had thanked Owens, and the sheriff had touched his hat brim to acknowledge the thanks before turning back toward town.

Longarm stood up in his stirrups now, trying to pick the easiest course across the earthen covering which in the virtually rainless, snowless country was still spread in loose clumps over the undisturbed soil beyond the downgrade. At the end of the layer of raw dirt he could make out dim signs of a fork in the trail. There were three or four rectangular areas in the fork that obviously had been cleared at one time to provide leveled spaces for houses. The area around the house foundations was strewn with bits and pieces of broken board-ends and small heaps of unidentifiable debris left behind when the houses had been moved.

"It don't look too bad, old son," Longarm said into the sunny air as he reined his horse down the incline and past

163

the deserted homesites. "Just keep on moving slow and easy. You can't have much further to go now."

In that desert country where rain was a rarity and which was almost totally barren of vegetation, Longarm had little trouble following the hoof-pocked trace. In some short stretches the trail ran as straight as a string. In others it wound in and out to avoid small yawning crevasses or the humps of low hillocks. The erratic course that the terrain imposed slowed Longarm's progress, and he'd been in the saddle for almost another quarter of an hour before he sighted the vee of a roof-peak above the broken land ahead.

"Well, old son," Longarm commented. "It sure looks like you've found the place you been aiming for. If that ain't old Jim Allen's place, I'll be a monkey's uncle."

Touching his mount's flank with a light boot-toe prod, Longarm kept his eyes on the roof-peak until he could see the entire ridge of the shingled roof and on high spots in the trail could also sight a portion of one wall. He toe-prodded the horse to a faster gait, and bit by bit the cabin ahead was revealed.

Longarm swiveled his head from side to side to survey the area around the cabin as he drew closer to it. The terrain was not rough or badly broken, but the stretches of loose yellow sandy soil around the little building had been blown into long rows of uneven ripples by the intermittent hot gusting winds. He did not see the sprawled body of a man stretched motionless on the barren expanse until he was within fifty or sixty yards of the little structure.

Reining in quickly, Longarm stayed in the saddle for a moment, staring at the inert figure. He shouted a hello, but there was still no sign of life from the cabin. He toed the horse ahead, and pulled up between the cabin and the outstretched form on the rippling surface of the barren ground. He made a quick survey of the landscape beyond the cabin, but saw no movement there either.

"Now, quit acting like a damn tenderfoot, old son," he muttered as he realized that the dead man could not have been killed during the short time he'd spent riding from Holbrook. "You oughta have brains enough to know that fellow over yonder wasn't cut down lately. If there'd been a gunfight after you left the railroad tracks, you'd've heard the shooting."

Toeing his mount into motion again, he reined it close to the sprawled body and dismounted. He kept his eyes moving between the prone figure lying in front of him and the cabin just beyond. His closer observation as he walked to stand beside the body told him four things. The first was that the body was too young to be that of the former postmaster he'd come looking for, nor did he recognize the dead man as being a wanted criminal. He was sure that the face of the corpse was not one that he'd encountered before, nor had he seen it on any wanted posters.

His next discovery was that the dead man had been killed by either one of two gunshots. There was a bullet hole in his left chest that had created a big circle of blood on his shirt, and another in his head just above one eye. Either bullet would have been instantly fatal. Longarm's third discovery was that the corpse had been lying where he'd found it for at least a day, but not much longer. The body was not frozen in the rigor mortis that follows death by a few hours and lasts half a day, and as yet it had not started to bloat or to deteriorate in the blazing Arizona sunshine.

However, his fourth discovery as he began searching the corpse was more puzzling than any of the first three.

Longarm found that the dead man did not have a gunbelt on, nor was there a weapon near his body. To satisfy himself that the man had been unarmed when he'd taken the fatal gunshot wounds, Longarm lifted the dead man's torso to see if there was a weapon under it. There was not. Deferring any further examination of the corpse until later, Longarm stepped over to the house and went in through its open front door.

Total wreckage was the only description that Longarm could think of for the scene that met his eyes. Rarely had he seen such chaotic destruction in one small room. Three of the four straight chairs it contained had been overturned. So had an easy chair at one side of the room. The mattress from the single bedstead that stood opposite the door below the room's one window had been dragged off the springs and lay humped on the floor.

Jagged cracks radiated from bullet holes in the mirror of a tall six-drawer bureau that rose against the wall beyond the bed. Its drawers had been pulled out of the frame. They lay overturned on the bare floorboards, their contents— jeans, shirts, underwear, socks—in tangled heaps on the floor nearby.

One end of the narrow two-burner stove that stood opposite the bedstead across the room had been pulled away from the wall at a sharp angle. It had carried the stovepipe with it. Black flakes of soot strewed the top of the stove and the stew pot and frying pan that lay nearby as well as the floor around them.

Blurred boot-prints showed on the soot-covered floor all around the circular table that occupied the center of the room. All of them had such raggedly defined outlines that it was impossible for Longarm to tell one from another or even to distinguish right foot from left foot. He could get nothing more than a vague idea of how many men had been involved in the fracas.

"Could of been two, could of been three," he muttered. "Or maybe even four. There just ain't no real way to tell, old son. But maybe if you look at them prints real close, you might be able to match 'em up with some that's likely on the ground outside. And you better try extra hard, because your next job's going to be tracking down whoever was mixed up in this fracas."

As he bent forward for a second and closer look at a set of boot-prints near the humped soot-covered mattress, Longarm's jaw dropped in surprise when in the inverted vee of the mattress-edge he saw a man's hand and an inch or two of wrist lying motionless on the floor beneath it. Getting to his feet, Longarm lifted the mattress away.

For a moment Longarm gazed at the dead man, his brow knitted in a silent frown. Then he hunkered down and began studying the face of the second corpse he'd discovered so unexpectedly.

"One thing's for certain," he muttered after a moment spent examining the wrinkled face and sparse gray hair of the corpse. "Whoever this fellow was, he sure wasn't no spring chicken. And he wasn't no ranch hand neither. Them hands of his is softer'n a baby's butt. Now if you ain't making a mighty wrong guess, old son, he's got to be the man that owned this house, Jim Allen that used to be the postmaster in Holbrook."

Reaching into the dead man's shirt pockets, Longarm found them empty. He tackled the next job, of probing into the front pockets of the jeans which were the corpse's only other garment. Slipping his hand into the front pockets, he

167

found a Barlow knife in one. His search of the second produced a few coins: three silver dollars, two half-dollars, and a twenty-five-cent piece.

Dropping the coins to the floor beside the knife, Longarm turned the body on its side and reached into the hip pocket nearest him. His fingers encountered soft thin cloth. He grasped it and pulled out a faded blue bandanna. He dropped the kerchief to explore the last remaining pocket, and his probing fingers told him that it contained only some sort of paper.

Longarm wriggled his fingertips and crossed and recrossed his forefinger and index finger trying to get a firm grip on the slippery paper. At last he succeeded in pulling it from the pocket and looked down at it. His crossed fingertips were holding two triangles of paper. One was the white corner torn from an envelope. The other triangle could have come from only one source. It bore the corner of an imprinted scrollwork border that had unmistakably been torn from United States currency, for on it was printed "$100." Turning the scrap over, he saw the same imprint on the reverse in a darker shade of green.

"Well, now, old son," Longarm said, his voice loud in the silence of the little room. "It looks like you've finally struck some pay dirt."

Turning his eyes back to the triangular bits of paper and turning the white scrap over, Longarm saw now that this piece had an imprint of its own, the capital letter S and a curve which could only be the upper portion of lowercase E.

"I'd bet a blind man dollars to doughnuts the rest of that piece of paper come off of an envelope from the Security Bank down in Phoenix," Longarm muttered. "Both of 'em must've torn free when whoever killed this Allen fellow was worming it outta his hip pocket. And there just might be something more here in this cabin or on that dead man laying outside that'd give you a lead to running down whoever done these killings."

Levering himself to his feet, Longarm made a second examination of the little cabin to be sure he was not overlooking some detail or bit of evidence that might help him. The search was disappointing. Though he worked more slowly and much more carefully, no new find rewarded him. Aside from the sparse supply of flour, sugar, and coffee stored in the stove's small oven, and the gaggle of clothing that lay beside the bureau, he found nothing else.

"Well, you done half your job, old son. Now, there ain't a bit of use wasting time looking around in here, because it's dollars to doughnuts that you ain't going to find much that'd help you. But you didn't stop long enough at that other fellow's body to turn out his pockets, so you better go do that. Then you can finish up in town and come back out here to scout around for a trail you can pick up."

Longarm stepped outside and began the unpleasant task of going through the pockets of the dead man he'd first encountered. There was nothing in his shirt pockets but a few drying cigars and a fistful of matches. His trousers pockets yielded a small roll of currency and a dollar or less of loose change. Longarm counted the roll of bills. To his surprise, it totaled more than five hundred dollars.

"Now, that settles him as being some kinda outlaw," Longarm muttered as he riffled through the bills. "Nobody but them carries this kinda money, or even got this much money."

Rolling the limp corpse over on its face, Longarm began exploring the hip pockets of the dead man's jeans. One contained a crumpled sweat-stiff bandanna. In the other pocket there was a fold of gray-hued cardboard.

Spreading the fold open, Longarm saw the standing figures of five men. They were standing close, their elbows locked together, in front of a photographer's studio backdrop. Three of them he recognized at once, and Longarm's eyebrows shot up in astonishment. The face in the center was that of Jim Allen, who lay dead on the floor of the cabin. The man on his left was the dead man whose body he'd just searched. The third was one that Longarm had seen on wanted posters many times, the notorious outlaw Johnny Ringo.

"Now who in tunket can them other ones be?" Longarm muttered as he studied the images in the picture. "And how'd that dead postmaster fellow Jim Allen get mixed up with any bunch that's got Johnny Ringo in it? If I ain't wrong, that's him sure as God made little green apples. Now, old son, it stands to reason that the bunch in this picture wasn't just strangers that got together to have their picture made. There's a lot of things this here picture might mean because it just don't jibe, that dead postmaster being in a picture with them outlaws. Before you start out looking for any of 'em that's still alive, you better find out all you can here in Holbrook, and the man you better ask is Sheriff Commodore Perry Owens."

Less than two minutes later, Longarm was in the saddle of his livery horse, nudging it to a distance-eating canter on the trail back to Holbrook.

# Chapter 14

"Well, Sheriff Owens, I'm real glad you could put a name to that outlaw I never had run across before," Longarm said. "I don't recall seeing the name of that fellow you said was Pony Deal on our wanted list, though."

"I hope my memory served me correctly, Longarm," Owens said. "But I'm sure that dead man you found out at Jim Allen's shack was Pony Deal. He was just a tinhorn gambler that ran errands for the real crooks."

"Then I don't reckon it'd be easy to make a case against him, even providing he was alive," Longarm said. "But I'd imagine he got a little split of the loot from the ones that did the real work."

"I'll have to agree with you about that," Owens said.

"It ain't likely that Allen'd have gone along on stickups and such-like with them fellows that killed him and Pony Deal," Longarm observed. "But he had to know a lot about 'em, to be handling their money. Maybe they cut him and Deal down to keep 'em from talking too much."

"That's been known to happen," the sheriff agreed. "And Jim Allen wouldn't've been much use to them once he left the post office."

"It ain't likely we'll know, unless I run down the other scoundrels that come here to get rid of Allen." Longarm's voice was low-pitched and thoughtful, as it tended to be when he was thinking aloud. "And the trail them fellows who was there with Pony Deal left is likely too cold to pick up and follow now. But what I can't keep from thinking about is that bank down in Phoenix that was handling all that money for 'em."

"You don't think a big bank like that would be tied in with a bunch of crooks, do you?" Owens said.

"Now, that ain't what I'm getting at," Longarm replied. "It don't stand to reason a big outfit like that bank is would get wound up with outlaws that robs banks all the time."

"What're you getting at then?" the sheriff asked.

"Outlaws stick together," Longarm replied. "If one of 'em happens to be having a bad time, there's one of their own kind standing ready to give 'em a hand to tide 'em over. And the easy way for them to pass money along is to have a bank send it."

"But how'd they get the money to the bank?"

"That's what I been asking myself," Longarm replied. "And what comes to mind is they got to have a hideout close to the bank. I'll put it to you that there ain't no better hidey-hole for outlaws than a place like that big Apache reservation."

"But the army—" Owens began.

Longarm cut him short, saying, "The army's got a handful riding herd on the Apaches, and the Apaches keep busy trying to get away from the army. As I see

172

it, the outlaws would have things pretty much their own way down to the south part of that big reservation."

"I hadn't looked at it that way before, but I'm damned if I don't believe your idea's a good one," Owens told him.

"Well, it ain't going to take me long to find out," Longarm said. "From what I seen while I was on the way here from Phoenix, there's a lot more reservation than there is Apaches."

"Too much rough country, I'd say," Owens replied. "I get the idea you'll be heading for the reservation then, before you go back to Denver?"

"I still ain't closed my case till I find out who was in that bunch that come up here to kill the fellow that used to be postmaster. From the footprints I looked at out at his cabin, there was two of 'em, maybe three."

"Meaning you're going to try tracking them down?"

"Well, was you standing in my boots, wouldn't you?"

Owens was silent for a moment, then he nodded. "I suppose I would, Longarm. And I'd like nothing better than to be going with you, but I can't just walk away from my job here."

"And I'd like to have you along when I'm chasing after them, but it's my case to close. Now, if Billy Vail sends me a wire it'll be in care of your office, so you just send him one saying I'm heading that way, but I'm taking a sorta roundabout road. And any time you got a case around Denver, I won't be forgetting I owe you a favor."

"You don't owe me a thing, Longarm, but I'll keep it in mind," Owens replied. "And the Santa Fe's been hinting that they'd like to have me on their railroad detective force, so you might see me sooner than you expect."

As the dark blue that followed an orangy-red sunset continued to move westward across the sky, Longarm began reining his horse in at shorter and shorter intervals. As he'd done each time he'd stopped earlier, he stood up in his stirrups and scanned the barren land ahead, looking for the hint of green that promised a stream or a water hole.

"Old son," he said, his voice sounding loud in the windless air, "that dabble of water you still got ain't going to be enough for you and the horse too. And if your luck ain't better tomorrow, it's going to be a real dry day."

Dropping down into his saddle once more, he toed the tiring animal ahead. The sky was steadily taking on a deeper hue now, in the sudden change from daylight to darkness that marked the desert country. Longarm knew that he had only a little time left to find a place where he could shelter for the night, and he was also aware that he had to find water before dark or he'd be forced to make a dry camp. He continued to peer ahead, hoping that he'd beat the approaching night.

A low buttress of striated rock looming above the level soil ahead caught Longarm's eyes as he topped a long gentle upslope. "Now, that's just the place you need for a good night's rest, old son," he said. "That little hump don't look like such a much, and it ain't likely there'll be no more water there than there is anyplace else, but them big cracks in it'll cut the night wind a mite, and that's better'n nothing."

Longarm reined his horse toward the small mesa. He'd covered about half the distance to it when lead whistling only a few inches away from his ear, followed by the high-pitched splat of the rifle shot, warned him that he'd become the target for an ambusher. As he started to slide from his saddle he reached for his Winchester, intending to draw, turn, and snapshot at the bushwhacker. Then the reaction of survival which after so many close brushes with death had become second nature to him dictated a different move almost automatically.

Longarm crumpled and toppled from the saddle. As he half-fell and half-slid from the horse, he grabbed for the butt of his Winchester and managed to get a grip on it firm enough to yank it free and carry it to the ground with him. He twisted as he was falling so that he'd land belly down, in a position that let him tilt his chin up at an angle which would allow him to turn his eyes in the direction from which the shot came.

Through slitted lids Longarm watched the thin wraith of powder smoke dissipate above the top of the mesa. He'd been sweeping his eyes across the featureless terrain for only a moment, scanning the face and rim of the high striated rock formation, when his attacker stood up. He was silhouetted against the sky, a rifle in his hand. Longarm brought his Winchester's muzzle around, and had the man in his sights when he decided that he needed information more than he did the lifeless body of his still-unknown attacker.

Gambling that the few moves he'd need would not be noticed by his attacker, Longarm slowly lowered his rifle to the ground and lay motionless, watching. For a few moments the man on the mesa stood still. Through the crystal-clear desert air Longarm could see

175

his head moving as he swung it from side to side, obviously trying to decide if Longarm had been riding alone or if he had others with him. There being no one else to see, and no movement by Longarm to alarm him, the sniper on the ridge of the mesa turned away and disappeared below the rim of the rock formation.

Knowing that his life might depend on his ability to remain motionless, Longarm did not stir. He waited, not knowing whether or not he was still visible to the man who'd tried to kill him. The patience which had become a habit in situations such as he was in at the moment was rewarded after a surprisingly short wait. The man who'd tried to kill him came back into sight. This time he was on horseback, reining toward Longarm.

Though the minutes seemed to drag into hours while he waited, Longarm held his place. He moved slowly, and only enough to slip his hand to the butt of his holstered Colt as he heard the distant muffled hoofbeats of his attacker's horse draw closer. In spite of the temptation to shift his position enough to get a glimpse of the oncoming rider, Longarm remained motionless.

Steadily the hoofbeats grew louder. Then they stopped. The unmistakable creaking of saddle leather told Longarm that his attacker was dismounting. Then the soft crunch of boots on the sandy soil gave him the clue he needed. Longarm waited, judging the man's distance by the sound of his steps until he decided the time for action had come.

Longarm's judgment had been excellent. He opened his eyes as he whipped out his Colt and jammed it upwards until it was stopped by the gun's muzzle jamming into the sniper's chin.

"I ain't of a mind to pull trigger right now," Longarm said quickly. "But was I you, I'd just keep my hands from getting itchy to draw, because before you grab the butt of your pistol, your head'll be blown plumb off your neck."

For a moment the man did not speak, and when he did his voice was garbled by the pressure of Longarm's pistol muzzle. At last he managed to gasp, "All right. You got me. Now tell me what the hell you're after."

"All I want right this minute's a little conversation," Longarm replied. "First you tell me who you are, then you tell me why you was sniping at me."

"Bill Brown's my name," the man replied. "And I didn't know from Adam's off-ox who you was. When I started up here from Douglas, coming back from a job I had on a ranch down in Mexico, just about everybody I talked to said I'd better shoot first and ask questions later, on account of there's wild Apaches and outlaws hiding out all over the place."

Longarm had been a lawman long enough to be able to distinguish truth from a lie. He released the pressure of his Colt and holstered it, then said, "You're right as rain about there being a lot of outlaws loose on this damn desert, along with a big bunch of extra-mean Apaches."

"I don't happen to be either one of them," young Brown snapped. "And we're moving in different directions, so you head your way and I'll go along on mine."

"Hold on just a minute, now," Longarm said quickly. "I don't reckon you're in such a hurry that you can't take time to answer me a question or two."

"What kind of questions?"

"My name's Long, Custis Long." Longarm was taking out his wallet as he spoke. He opened it and displayed his badge as he went on. "And like this badge says, I'm a deputy United States marshal. I'm sorry if I rubbed you the wrong way."

"Well, I guess I asked for it, shooting at you like a tenderfoot without knowing who you are. Now, go ahead and ask your questions. What're you trying to find out?"

"Just if you've seen anybody or even any sign that there's been two or maybe three men passing or making camp around here lately."

For a moment young Brown frowned thoughtfully. Then he replied, "I can't be sure about that, Marshal Long. I thought I saw some smoke back along the way a few miles, but I couldn't be sure. It didn't last but a few minutes, and I didn't have any landmark to find it by again."

"You'd be bound to know east from west," Longarm suggested.

"It was generally eastward, maybe a little to the south."

"But you never got a good look at it or seen anybody?"

Brown shook his head as he replied, "Nary a soul. It was a pretty good stretch off. East and a little bit to the south."

"That's all I need to know," Longarm said. "So I'll push on that way, and I guess you'd like to get moving again too."

"I sure would. I've got a long way to go to get home."

Longarm raised his hand in a gesture of farewell and started for his horse. Brown moved in the opposite direction. Neither of them looked back.

When Longarm saw the almost-invisible smoke trail curling up against the cloudless blue sky of late afternoon, he reined in. The thin gray line was dissipating almost as

178

soon as it became visible in its rise above the horizon. Sliding one of his long thin cigars out of his pocket, Longarm flicked his thumbnail across a match-head and puffed until the tip of the cheroot glowed red.

After he'd enjoyed a few inhalations he said into the empty desert air, "It looks like you've got to where you was heading, old son. Just as sure as God made little green apples, was you to draw a straight line from here to that smoke-trace you'd wind up in Tombstone in about two more days. And sure as God made little green apples, that's where somebody that's heading for Tombstone has stopped for the night."

Toeing his horse ahead, Longarm kept his eyes fixed on the wavering line of smoke. As the pale blue of daylight sky beyond it deepened into darkness, the stars became his guide. Familiar with the deceptiveness of distance in the clean thin desert air, Longarm set a pace that would get him to his destination in the moments when the first deceptive dusk began to shroud the barren ground.

By the time he reached a point where he could see the glow of a small campfire's coals silhouetting the figures of two men hunkered down, the startlingly sudden desert darkness had set in. Longarm pulled up his horse and dropped the reins to the ground to assure himself that the horse would stand.

Then he swung out of his saddle and began a slow approach toward the small fire. He pressed each foot down firmly to pack the loose arid soil before leaning forward to put his weight on it. When Longarm could hear the voices of the men, but was still unable to make out what they were saying, he stopped for a moment and tried to get an idea of their low-voiced conversation.

Longarm's plan failed to live up to his expectations. The man who did most of the talking had a hoarse voice pitched just above a whisper. Longarm could catch only an occasional word of what he was saying until the man who'd been largely silent broke into one of his companion's low-voiced discourses.

"Now damn it, Billy, you hold up before you swig down another swallow of that damn whiskey!" he burst out. "You ain't going to push off none of that Holbrook mess on me! Damn it, I didn't pick out Pony Deal to go along with us! It was you done that!"

"Was I trying to make like I didn't?" his companion said, raising his voice for the first time. "And I sure didn't hear you saying nothing about Pony not being welcome up there!"

"Well, you heard what that old fart that was the postmaster such a long time said about him!"

"Damn it, he never said a word to me about him and Pony fussing over the split-up we been making! And that's the truth or my name ain't Billy Claiborne!"

"Pony sure as hell said a lot to me!"

"Then why didn't you pass it on?"

"Because I didn't aim to rile you up! And besides, I figured you was the boss and picked him out on account of you and him was kinfolks!"

"Kinfolks don't count with me where money's concerned!"

"Like hell it don't! You damn Claibornes is as bad as the Clantons!"

"And you Coes is worse! Now don't you—"

But Coe's tirade was beyond stopping. His voice raised to a rasping shout that drowned his companion's effort to speak. "If you wasn't such a greedy Claiborne son of a bitch you'd've made sure we was doing like we said we would, share and share alike!"

Seeing that the argument between the two outlaws was heading for a showdown that would certainly end in a gunfight, Longarm intervened. He drew his Colt and let off a shot into the fire, sending small arcs of glowing red coals flying up in sparkling red arcs.

"Drop them guns, both of you!" he called, shouting loudly enough to drown out the voices of the two angry outlaws. "My name's Long, and I'm a—"

Longarm's effort to break up the impending gunfight came an instant too late. Both Claiborne and Coe ignored the shot he'd fired. They did not even glance at Longarm, for they were now too intent on killing one another.

Claiborne fell first. He lurched to the ground as his shot went wild, but still had enough life remaining to get Coe in his sights and trigger off a shot. Then Coe buckled and sagged and sank slowly to the ground. He lurched forward and went to his knees, his head and arms drooping. His knees gave way and he dropped to lie in a motionless sprawl as Claiborne's revolver fell from his hand. Then Claiborne's head sagged and he crumpled into a lifeless heap, his useless revolver lying beside his unmoving form.

During the three or four seconds the gunfight had lasted, Longarm had not fired another shot, but he still held his Colt. His hands moved very slowly as he flipped out the revolver's chamber and replaced the spent round with a fresh one.

"Well, old son," he said at last into the desert silence, "it ain't real often that you run into a pair of outlaws that's so set on killing each other that they don't pay any attention to you. But it looks like your case is closed, and it ain't a minute too soon. All you got to do now is find a sheriff and tell him he's got a mess to clean up out here, and then you can catch a train and head back to Denver. And you better pick out a slow train, because by the time you get there, Billy Vail's certain sure to have a new case for you."

Watch for

**LONGARM AND THE UTE NATION**

158th in the bold
LONGARM series from Jove

*Coming in February!*